BRIGHT MORNING
by
Jan Hathaway

Author of "THE COMING OF EAGLES" *and*
"ROBYNN'S WAY"

It was an unpleasant surprise to Laura Gray to receive, without preparation or warning, the news that her widowed mother had remarried the dean of the junior college where Mrs. Gray taught. It was even more disturbing to realize that her own disturbed emotional attitude was preventing Laura from setting a good example to the handicapped children at the summer camp where the fifteen-year-old was serving as a counselor.

In an attempt to straighten out her tangled thoughts, Laura resigned her position and fled to the solitude of the home temporarily deserted by her honeymooning parent, only to be recalled to meet the challenge of caring for a blind girl who, even like herself, was striking out at the world because she personally was unhappy.

A story for teen-agers past, present and future.

For
Lynn Popham
with affection

BRIGHT MORNING

BRIGHT MORNING

by

JAN HATHAWAY

Alouette Romance
By
Sharon Publications, Inc.
Closter, NJ

Copyright © MCMLXIV by Arcadia House
Published by
Sharon Publications Inc.
Closter, N.J. 07624
Printed in the U.S.A.
Cover illustrations by Kim Mulkey
ISBN 0-89531-139-9

BRIGHT MORNING

Chapter 1

Warren Wittwer said that if no one could find his leg braces, he would just have to stay at the camp all summer. He smiled triumphantly, a handsome ten-year-old with curly blond hair and the bluest eyes Laura Gray had ever seen. He told her proudly: "I thunk that up all by myself. Ain't that somethin'?"

It was difficult for Laura not to smile back. Somehow, though, she managed to bring a stern expression to her face. "In my opinion," she announced, "you've goofed. Suppose a raccoon steals those braces? Or suppose you can't remember where you hid them? Do you think it'll be fun to spend all summer in a wheel chair?"

She might just as well have saved her breath. Warren bent contentedly over the leather belt he was making for his father. "Wheel chairs ain't so bad," he argued. "Anyhow, Camp Mosher's better'n the city."

Laura looked at her wristwatch. For a moment she felt so panicky she came dangerously close to running to Miss Humbert for help. After all, she thought, Master Warren Wittwer just *had* to be shipped out on the eleven o'clock bus. His family would be expecting him in San Francisco at two-thirty. And what about the new boy who was coming that afternoon to take Warren's place in Cabin 3?

But the panicky feeling disappeared almost as quickly as it had come. Keeping her voice gentle and calm, Laura argued back: "The thing that bothers me most is the black mark you're putting on your record. With or without your braces, you'll leave this morning, that's for sure. But if you leave with a black mark on your record, you won't be allowed to come back next year. All the other boys of Cabin 3 will be back, but not you."

"Yeah?"

"Yes."

He swallowed hard.

Laura made a joke of the whole thing. "Braces, braces," she called, "who's got the braces?"

Warren Wittwer startled her. "I don't care," he said. "Next year ain't this year, is it?"

Warren Wittwer, you behave!"

If he noticed the iron in her voice, he gave no sign. He selected a diamond-shaped punch from the punch rack and set it just so on the broad leather belt. Holding the punch absolutely straight, he picked up the wooden mallet and gave the punch four brisk taps. The diamond imprint left in the leather was perfect, the upper and lower points exactly lined up with the points of the other diamonds he had imprinted along the top border of his design. He was a remarkably good craftsman, Laura decided. She made a mental note to include that observation in the final report she would have to write about him that evening.

But as for his sense of discipline!

"One more chance," she warned him. "I can be tough when I have to be."

"Miss Laura?"

"Yes?"

"How old are you?"

"Practically sixteen. Why?"

"Ain't it awful," he giggled, "to be old? Ma always says so."

Quickly, still keeping her face stern but her manner calm, Laura did what she had to do. She got behind Master Warren Wittwer and lifted him from the bench and carried him to his bunk in Cabin 3. She set him down, dropped to a crouch, and began to take off his left shoe. Naturally, all conversation stopped as the five other boys watched from their bunks or wheel chairs.

By the time Laura had gotten the socks, shoes, shirt and undershirt off, Master Warren Wittwer was ready to think things over. "Hey," he protested, "I ain't no baby!"

"I think you are. Now relax, there's my precious little baby! Laura will carry you and bathe you and dress you and give you a lollipop to suck on the bus."

Somebody behind Laura snickered. Next, all the boys began to laugh. Finally, two boys began to chant: "Warren's a baby, Warren's a baby . . ." And that chanting, by golly, clinched the victory!

Red-faced and angry, Warren screeched, "Under the cabin! I put 'em under the cabin!"

"Smarty pants!"

Warren screeched: "I hate you! I hate you!"

Laura refused to take the tantrum seriously. She gave him a smacking kiss on the cheek and retorted, "Well, I love you, so there!"

Humming, feeling hugely pleased because she had handled the problem unaided, Laura left the cabin on the trot. She found Keith Moller still cleaning up the grounds before Cabin 7, and she volunteered to do the raking for him if he would get those pesky braces out from under Cabin 3. Keith, as usual, had to tease her. "That isn't much of a trade for me, you know." Keith stood the rake against a redwood sapling and took a handkerchief from the back pocket of his denim trousers and wiped his perspiring face.

"Pat," Laura said. "Never wipe."

"Oh?"

"From time to time," she said airily, "I'll give you such little tips on how to become a civilized gentleman."

"I'd rather have some dances from time to time."

"Not with me, Keith. Ask anyone. When a boy leads me thisaway, I usually go thataway."

"Not, I've noticed, when you're dancing with Clay Chatham."

Long before the blush came, Laura could feel it coming.

The nice thing about Keith Moller, though, was that he knew the difference between teasing and tormenting a person. "Sit and rest," he said. "You don't have to make deals with me just to get some help. Who gets the braces?"

"Warren Wittwer. Oh, and he should have a shower, Keith, before he dresses. Clay was supposed to be back by now, but he isn't, and it's getting late."

"One scrubbed Wittwer coming up!"

Laura waited just long enough to hear Warren Wittwer's first howl of outrage. After it had rung out like a bugle blare, Laura trotted on through the redwood forest to her own unit. She soon discovered that she might just as well have spared herself the exertion. On this scorching hot day in the San Lorenzo Valley of the Santa Cruz Mountains, all twenty girls in her unit were making like bumps on a log. Ten were actually napping on their bunks, four were reading in shaded places, and the other six were either listening to the radio or writing letters or both. At eleven o'clock, of course, all the girls would somehow get enough energy together to put on their bathing suits for their morning swim. In the meantime, they were clearly content to be where they were and to do what they were doing.

Delighted, Laura went on to the cabin she shared with Nikki McCloud. She joined Nikki on the little railed porch and settled down in one of the wicker chairs with a sense of having accomplished a great deal. "Next year," she told Nikki, "I think I'll apply for work in a boys' unit. Those types in Clay's unit are darned cute and interesting. I think they'd be fun to handle."

"There are problems enough in a unit for girls. Now hear this! There's a thief in this unit."

"There always is. This is my third year at Camp Mosher, and every year there's at least one thief in each unit. According to Miss Aronstam, that's to be expected. Most of the children come from underprivileged homes. I mean, money's really scarce in those homes. So sooner or later something is stolen."

"You mean you're not scandalized?"

"Nope."

"Well, I'm definitely scandalized. And with your permission, glorious muck-a-muck, I intend to catch the thief and make an example of her."

"Relax, Nikki."

"Suppose someone tells Miss Humbert?"

Laura looked at Nikki unbelievingly. Fortunately, she remembered before she laughed that this was Nikki's first season at Camp Mosher. "You'd be surprised," she told Nikki, "if you knew how much Miss Humbert knows about what's going on around here. First of all, Miss Humbert's a senior at the University of California. That means she's no fool. Next, Miss Humbert's studying to be a social worker. That means she has a pretty good idea of what makes people tick. And third but not least, Miss Humbert has her own way of getting information about what goes on in this division. Catch?"

"Just the same—"

But that was when Clay Chatham came back from Kenyon at last with the day's mail.

A tall, muscular towhead who was handsome and knew it, Clay got out of the red pickup truck and called imperiously to Nikki, "Hop or pop."

Nikki, pathetically, hopped. Blushing and all jittery, Nikki rushed down the stoop and straight over to Clay. Clay looked her up and down as if she were on inspection and then said, "You get better-looking all the time, Nikki. Maybe some evening soon I'll give you a break."

He gave Nikki three letters.

Then, his smile almost devilish, Clay looked straight at Laura and crackled, "Hop or pop."

"Pop."

Clay's smile faded. A look of genuine bewilderment came into his gray eyes. "What's eating you?" he asked. "Did my kids give you a rugged time?"

Suddenly, for a reason she did not understand, Laura wanted to humiliate him as he had just humiliated Nikki McCloud. She said flatly and firmly, "I don't like the way you treat too many people, Clay. You dance well, I'll concede that. But that doesn't give you the right to come here or anywhere else and tell people to hop or pop. Suppose *you* hop for a change, and right now. If you're the mail boy around here, deliver my letters, please."

Clay turned sunset red. Nikki made queer, strangling sounds in her throat. Clay turned and started to climb into the truck. Nikki, always a loyal friend, cried out hastily, "Clay, she's just tired, that's all."

Clay backed down from the truck. Evidently utterly unaware that his deliberate humiliation of Nikki had changed things, Clay called, "Hop over and apologize, Laura. I haven't got all day."

Laura just held her hand out for her mail and waited.

"Look," Clay said, "I'm willing to give you a break, but don't get high and mighty with me."

"Clay, if you don't deliver my mail, I'll talk to Miss Humbert. Who do you think you are to make people come running to you and all but beg for their mail?"

Their eyes locked.

Interestingly, his were the first to fall. "Don't bother me no more," Clay growled, but he did step over and hand Laura a letter. Without a single word more, all his movements stiff, Clay then got back into the truck and drove on to the next unit of Division III.

Nikki let her breath out in a long, long sigh. "You shouldn't have done that," Nikki said. "Clay likes you a lot. He told me."

Quite unperturbed—in fact, rather pleased with the way she had taught Clay something about consideration for others—Laura looked at the re- turn address her mother had printed so elegantly on the envelope. "Jolly England." She laughed. "It seems so strange to get a letter all the way from England. Probably Queen Elizabeth wants me to dash right over for a cup of tea in Buckingham Palace."

Nikki, it seemed, had a one-track mind this sizzling July day. "It's just Clay's way," Nikki excused him. " He doesn't mean half of what he says."

"All for one and one for all. And if you want some free advice, don't jump the second he asks you to dance with him this evening. And he *will* ask you to dance, if I know Clay, if only to teach me a lesson."

Laura slid her forefinger under the flap and opened the envelope. It was a one-side-of-one-sheet letter, she discovered. Such a lazy mother hen! Such a skimpy reply to the five-page letter she had sent the mother hen last week! Just for that—

Laura never finished the thought. Her quick gray eyes came to fantastic words, words so fantastic she wondered if her vision were playing tricks on her. Teeth clenching her lower lip, Laura reread the words: "So Dr. Glenn Hansen and I were married yesterday, Laura, and you have a new father. . . ."

"Say," Nikki called, "what gives? You're so white it isn't comical!"

Laura forced a smile and tried to speak, but no words came.

"You mean," Nikki joshed, "that Queen Elizabeth really *did* invite you to tea? Fancy that!"

Somehow Laura got the letter back into the envelope. A great store of rage and bitterness swept through her, loosening her tongue. "Congratulate me," she ordered harshly. "I have a new father, Nikki; isn't that grand? That's why Mom wouldn't take me to England with her. She went over there to marry Dr. Hansen on the sly."

"*What?*"

Head down, a sickness in her stomach, tears in her eyes, Laura Gray ripped the envelope and letter into bits and rushed to her bunk in the cabin.

Chapter 2

Oddly enough, it was Clay Chatham who ended the weeps in the cabin. Clay thumped on the door at around eleven o'clock and hollered that Warren Wittwer wanted to say goodbye. Laura hollered back that she despised Dr. Glenn Hansen and Clay Chatham and Warren Wittwer and every other male on earth. Clay bellowed with laughter. "You sound just like those kids yelling they hate everyone who doesn't give them their way."

Into Laura's mind popped a memory of the red-faced anger of Warren Wittwer not too long before. Laura rushed into the bathroom to inspect her own face. Her face filled her with shame. She filled the sink with cold water and buried her face in the water five times, each time holding her breath for as long as she possibly could. The last two times she held her eyes open, hoping that the cold water would get the red streaks out of her eyeballs.

And Clay Chatham thumped on.

When Laura finally got outdoors, the big yellow bus was just rolling away. Clay, seated on the stoop of her cabin, was quick to say there was no harm done, ten-year-old kids being what they were. Still, Laura had the ghastly feeling that she had let Warren Wittwer down.

Guiltily, Laura gazed about Unit 3. Not a girl could be seen anywhere, and she had to chuckle. "All my girls are fish this year," she told Clay. "If I suggest a hike they say they're too tired. If I suggest a plant-study class they say they're too tired. But when eleven o'clock or three o'clock rolls around, then everybody jumps into a swimsuit and heads for the pool."

"Natch. It's the same with the boys in my unit, and there's a good reason for it, a good psychological reason, according to Miss Humbert."

"Such as?"

Clay shrugged. "Well," he explained, "according to Miss Humbert, almost anyone enjoys doing whatever he does pretty good."

"I don't think Miss Humbert said 'pretty good.' "

"Stop making like the daughter of an English professor."

"Sorry."

Clay looked at her through narrowed eyelids. "You have a rough tongue sometimes, Goldilocks. You had no call to dress me down as you did."

"Maybe I'm just tired of arrogant fellows who believe they're God's gift to girls."

"If I personally carried every letter to every cabin, I'd wear my legs down to my knees. For your info, there are two hundred cabins for the patients and thirty-five cabins for the room-and-board staff. And some of the cabins are a quarter-mile from the camp roads."

"How interesting! I'm new here! I never in the world guessed there were so many cabins here!"

"That's what I meant when I said you have a rough tongue, Goldilocks. You don't have to be sarcastic. I know you're starting your third summer here. I was just explaining why I call for the able-bodied people to come to the truck for their mail."

"You don't have to yell for people to hop or pop. And you don't have to say to a nice girl like Nikki that maybe one of these days you'll give her a break. You specifically promised me that you'd be gallant to Nikki, and you aren't keeping your promise."

"What do you think I was doing—insulting her?"

"Of course you were!"

"Brother, are you ever loopy! Look, let me explain from A through Z. Nobody appreciates anything unless they think it's pretty special. All right. So by behaving as if I think I'm something special, I make a kid like Nikki appreciate me. All right. So then when I say to a kid like Nikki that maybe I'll give her a break, right away she's deeply thrilled. Isn't that logical?"

Laura rolled her eyes heavenward.

Clay frowned. "Life's confusing to guys, too," he confided. "Lots of times a guy doesn't secretly know even a little bit about a whole lot. Well, what's he supposed to do? All anybody can do is guess at the right answer and behave the way his mind tells him to. Isn't that logical?"

"Logical, logical, logical—why does everything have to be logical?"

"Anyhow," Clay said, and now his own tongue was rough, "that's how I think, and that's how I behave, and it isn't your place to correct me or to put me in the mutt-house if I don't do what you order. Also, I don't like it when someone threatens to tattle to Miss Humbert if I don't do things their way."

"All right."

"All right—what?"

"So now you've told me off and feel very, very manly, and three cheers for you. Anything else?"

"For Pete's sake, what's nipping you?"

"Nothing much, really. I just don't like it when

people deliberately humiliate others just to make a great big point to somebody else."

"I was doing no such thing!"

"Nikki adores you, a hundred others adore you, three cheers for the handsome Clay Chatham, but I *won't* go riding with you alone in that truck to watch the moon come up somewhere. Now punish me dreadfully! I don't care. I don't care. I don't neck. Is that crude enough for you?"

He never answered her at that particular time in that particular place. His sharp ears heard long before hers the spat of leather heels on the black-top service road. He stood up and was throwing pebbles at a nearby tan oak tree when Miss Humbert turned in through the gateway. Miss Humbert was carrying an oblong slab of redwood burl and looking most pleased about something. "Clay," she called, "come make yourself useful." Her wise brown eyes noticed their angry expressions, and, laughing, Miss Humbert added: "It does no good at all to spat with girls, Clay. Girls simply won't fade away into nothingness, and they simply won't be less beautiful than they are."

"She's loopy, Miss Humbert!"

With all the dignity she could muster, Laura walked away from Clay. "Miss Humbert," she asked, "are the boys at the University of California as juvenile as the boys at Kenyon High?"

Miss Humbert made a quite graceful jump, but her wiggling fingers barely grazed the Unit 3 sign on the gatepost. "Sometimes," Miss Humbert confided, "I wish I were two inches taller. Be a hero, Clay, will you?"

Clay got the Unit 3 sign down in jig time. He accomplished the feat by stepping up onto the triangular support corner of the split-rail fence. From that work platform it was no effort at all for him to slide the Unit 3 sign from the holding bar.

Handing the sign to Miss Humbert, Clay said: "Logical. My father says there's a logical way to do anything."

Prettily, Miss Humbert plucked at the side seams of her Bermuda shorts and dropped Clay a curtsey. "It's so grand," Miss Humbert said, "to be given these tips from time to time."

The next thing she did thrilled Laura. She picked up the oblong of redwood burl and turned it so that Laura could read the lettering. There, burnt beautifully into the burl, was the name Laura had pleaded that the unit be given! *Deer Fern Unit.* And see that crazy deer head up there near the right-hand corner!

"Actually," Miss Humbert told Laura, "yours was an excellent suggestion. Even Miss Aronstam agreed that when you say Cabin No. 3 of Unit No. 3 of Division III, you're apt to confuse yourself. So all the units will have names now. Probably we'll even figure out names for the divisions."

Laura watched proudly as the new sign was slid into place along the holding bar.

Clay said matter-of-factly, "It could be a crummier name, I guess. Frankly, though, I think of a deer fern as a weed. I mean, you find them practically wherever you find running water. For my unit, Miss Humbert, I want a better name than deer fern."

"It's up to you, Clay. Now go away somewhere, will you, please? I have business to discuss with the head of the Deer Fern Unit."

"It won't do you any good," Clay said positively. "She's loopy, Miss Humbert, no fooling."

Laura ignored the crack. She sat down on the top rail of the low, five-rail split-redwood fence. She cross her ankles and sat looking down at her sleek, lightly tanned legs until Clay had finally left. It was queer, Laura thought, how the physical problems of one year could sometimes become the physical assets of another year. Last year her legs had been a downright disgrace, the knees so fatty, the thighs so scrawny. Now—

"Did you survive the shock?" Miss Humbert asked softly. She joined Laura on the fence and gave a cute giggle as the rail squeaked under their combined weight. "Please reduce, she ordered Laura, "if you want to sit on fences with me!"

Laura shrugged and said that she had survived the shock and that she would be all right, thank you very much.

"Your mother telephoned Miss Aronstam, by the way. Miss Aronstam suggested that it might be well for you to get the first news by letter.

Miss Aronstam was right, of course. It must be a startling experience to acquire a new father so suddenly."

"Yes, ma'am."

"Of course," Miss Humbert said, "it will be a rich experience for both you and your mother. I can't imagine anything finer than the love and companionship of a man who means much to me. I suppose that's why we women marry and then cling to our men until death."

A stellar jay came in rising and falling flight across the clearing. It squawked harshly as it landed on the platform-feeder mounted on a redwood post before Laura's cabin. Laura thought with a part of her mind that no bird could possibly be lovelier than the stellar jay. From its feathery crest to the tip of its vivid blue tail, it suggested to her, at least, a rollicking, self-reliant bundle of sassiness that had much to be sassy about—especially the dreamy way the vivid blue shaded off into black around the head. But another part of her mind, the dominant part just then, was busy with another thought, a thought it could not accept. Finally she had to tell Miss Humbert frankly, "Having a new father can't be a rich experience for me, ma'am. I guess I have no right to judge. But marriage is supposed to be forever, not just until somebody dies. And Dad died trying to save my life in the ocean. And Mom should have remembered that, if you ask me, and she should have talked it over with me, too. After all, I'm supposed to talk over a lot less important things with her."

"You mustn't accuse your mother of disloyalty to your father, you know. Let's talk about that jay for just a moment. You love the jays, I know. Very well. Life goes on for that jay whether it loses its mate or doesn't whether its young survive or fail to. But it's a rough life alone, even for a jay. So in the fullness of time, life being like that, the jay finds a new mate if it's lucky. I imagine there've been times since your father's unfortunate death when life has been rather rugged for your mother. It can't be the easiest thing in the world to raise a daughter alone and at the same time broaden one's professional knowledge and earn the daily bread. I happen to know your mother fairly well, Laura. I've attended certain of her lectures at Kenyon Junior College, and I've read some of her papers in various magazines or journals devoted to the teacher's art. I can't believe she would ever be disloyal to your father or to you or that she would ever fail to do her very best to make you happy."

"Thank you, ma'am."

Miss Humbert turned, and it seemed to Laura that Miss Humbert's brown eyes bored deep into the remotest corners of her brain. "In other words," Miss Humbert asked, "you won't listen to me or think over what I've said or give your mother the benefit of a reasonable doubt?"

"She had no right!"

Miss Humbert's forehead pucked into wrinkles. After a long, thoughtful silence, Miss Humbert shook her brunette head. "I have to disagree with you," she said. "I think that any educated, well-intentioned woman has the right to do what she thinks best for herself and her daughter. Now look here, Laura: I've always liked you and respected you. You've always struck me as being a very nice and very sensible person. Don't compel me to change my opinion of you."

Not knowing what else to say, Laura said mumblingly, "Yes, ma'am."

Miss Humbert eased down from the fence. Her voice and manner underwent a change. "Well," she said cripsly, "duty is duty and all that. Why don't you take it easy until after lunch and then lead the crutches brigade on a hike through the woods? It's absolutely essential that our little darlings use their legs out here. Did you know that bones suffer calcium loss if they're rested too much?"

Laura nodded. Unable to think of anything more to say, she eased down from the fence, too, and returned to her cabin.

But Miss Humbert was all wrong, she thought hotly. Her mother *had* been disloyal, and the minute she could find a year-around paid job she would leave the camp for crippled children and she would leave her mother's house, too.

Chapter 3

For Laura, the rest of the week added up to a soggy blah. Fifteen new girls came to Deer Fern Unit on Tuesday morning, and getting them settled in was complicated by the fact that four were crybabies and three were spoiled pets who made practically no effort to do anything for themselves. Laura spent most of that day and half the night soothing the crybabies and helping the spoiled pets get to and from the different camp areas and even to the bathroom. With so much tension and unhappiness inside her, Laura found it difficult and certainly not rewarding to be gentle with the crybabies or patient with the spoiled pets.

Then, on Wednesday, there was an unpleasant

incident at the swimming pool. It began about twenty minutes after Laura had taken the lifeguard's chair. Some redheaded boy in the pool suddenly challenged everyone to play basketball. Several girls at once proceeded to tell the boy he was asking for the bitterest defeat of his life. Sides were chosen. Next, everyone was hollering a demand for Miss Laura to fetch the ball and the baskets and to act as referee. It took about five minutes to get the floating baskets moored into place at each end of the pool, and during those five minutes the youngsters steamed themselves up by chanting cheers and hurling insults at one another. The redheaded boy lost his temper, and twice Laura had to tell him sharply either to behave or leave the pool. The second time she rebuked the boy a very ugly gleam came into his green eyes. Had she been as alert as she ought to have been, she would have been warned by that ugly gleam to disqualify him at once. As it was, she just climbed back into her chair and blew the signal for the game to begin.

The redheaded boy was the first to reach the

ball she tossed into the water. He threw the ball to one of his teammates and then swam with mighty splashing strokes toward the goal being defended by one of the girls who had teased him: Derinda Poitz. When the ball was thrown to him, Derinda batted it away and laughingly teased him some more. "Couldn't catch an elephant, couldn't catch an elephant," Derinda chanted. The boy called her a dirty name, and then he charged her and swung his left fist, and his fist landed smack on her nose, and Derinda gave a scream and then sank.

Laura had to act fast, without time for thought. She made a beautiful dive that carried her well beyond some players swimming near her chair, and she hit the water cleanly, with a twist of her body that got her aimed in the direction of the spot at which Derinda had sunk. Five powerful strokes of arms and legs carried her to Derinda at the bottom of the pool and then, gripping Derinda by the hair, she kicked her way up to the surface. Naturally, with blood streaming from her nose and too much water sucked into her, Derinda panicked. By now all the kids were screaming, and several of the college girl division heads were coming to help out, but Laura had no way of knowing all that. Three times Derinda's fingernails raked Laura's face before she could get poor Derinda under control. Somehow, though, Laura at last got the girl up out of the pool. A brawny college fellow scooped Derinda up and hustled her off to the medical office. Three college girl division heads went to work quieting the kids in the pool. Miss Aronstam herself came to investigate and packed off the redheaded boy in a hurry.

That evening, of course, Laura was summoned to Miss Aronstam's office and was rebuked.

"My dear young lady," Miss Aronstam said forcefully, "you are not employed here to daydream or to sulk in the lifeguard's chair. When you're in that chair, you're in a position of trust. You're supposed to keep a sharp eye on the children, and it's certainly your duty to forestall troublemakers before trouble begins. I fail to understand why you neglected to discipline Vinnie Lowe when he lost his temper. And I fail to understand why, his ugly mood considered, you allowed him to participate in the basketball game."

"I just wasn't thinking," Laura admitted. "I suppose I assumed he'd settle down and behave once the fun got under way."

Miss Aronstam was short, quite thin, gray-haired woman who had the reputation of being somewhat peppery. She did not belie her reputation now.

"I dislike young women who neglect to think," she said sharply. "God certainly didn't give you brains for use as an ornament. I suggest you visit Derinda in our infirmary. Indeed, I order you to visit her. I want you to see what happens in a camp such as this when a person entrusted with responsibility neglects to think."

"Ma'am, I—"

Miss Aronstam interrupted by slapping the desk hard with the flat of her left hand. "I'll accept no excuses and no pointless apologies, Laura. A patient in our care might have drowned or had her nose broken. Had either of those things happened, the reputation of Camp Mosher might have suffered irreparable damage. Under the circumstances, I have no choice but to demote you. Effective tomorrow morning, Beverly Anglin will replace you as unit head. We'll shift Nikki McCloud to my staff, and you'll be Beverly's assistant. That will be all."

Laura, her lips trembling, just managed to get out of there before she could say something she might rue later on. She had to sit down in one of the lounge chairs before the mess hall, though, to get herself under some kind of control before she went to visit Derinda in the infirmary. Such weeks, Laura thought wildly, should not happen even to a skunk.

Then, on Saturday, things got even worse. Beverly Anglin quietly but firmly insisted that as the boss of the Deer Fern Unit, she had the right to expect Laura to keep the cabin they shared in perfect order. "After all," Beverly told her. "I've been working like a mule to get this unit in proper condition, and I just can't be expected to do everything."

Laura deemed that crack to be an insult. By that time, disgusted with the course her life seemed to be taking these days, Laura was in no mood to take anything more from anyone. She snapped hotly, "You've never worked in a neater, cleaner or happier unit of Camp Mosher, and you know it."

Quite tall and heavy for sixteen, Beverly jeered: "Oh, are you going to brawl with me now? Everybody's wrong except Laura Gray. Do you know what I truly think? I truly think you ought to get away from Camp Mosher and think things over. You practically snapped at every girl in the unit this morning. And let's be very clear about something while we're on *that* subject. I won't allow an assistant to snap at me when I give an order."

"In that case, Beverly, find yourself another assistant."

"Can do, will do."

Laura forced a snorting sort of laugh and just walked out and whammed the cabin door shut behind her. She stood looking around at the big circle of cabins, at a loss what to do next. But all the girls seemed busy enough, and Keith Moller had done his customary good job of raking the grounds clean and smooth and watering the ferns and shrubs in the plantings before each cabin. On an impulse, suddenly tired of people, Laura struck off across the circle until she had come to Big Tree Trail. One of the girls on crutches saw where she was headed and called: "Me, too, Miss Laura, me, too!" Laura just plain ignored her. She dogtrotted up the trail a good hundred feet before she slowed to a walk. By then she was well into the woods, and all the scrub oak and great redwoods and shrubs between her and the camp had the effect of muting the camp sounds so nicely it was hard to believe a great camp filled with kids was located so close.

But even on the trail her luck was bad. Near cute little Popham Brook, she met Nikki, of all people. Nikki whooped animatedly and raised her right hand and cried: "Hail." Nikki then sat down beside the brook and took off her socks and shoes. "Don't ever work right in Miss Aronstam's office,"

Nikki advised. "Talk about a regular pepperpot."

"Well, to be fair about it, she does enough work for five women. I guess I miss you, Nikki."

"I guess I miss you, too. I told Miss Aronstam. She asked me some questions about you, and I answered them. Then I remembered the demotion, and I told her right out that it was unfair."

Laura's eyes widened. "You didn't!"

Nikki lowered her feet into the brook. Nikki squealed and hauled her feet out in a hurry. "I'll freeze to death!" Nikki exclaimed. "I will!"

Chuckling, Laura grabbed one of the feet and tipped Nikki over backward and then slapped the sole of the foot with her fingertips. Nikki giggled and said the cure was worse than the ailment. Laura sat down beside Nikki, and Nikki just lay there as she was, a mass of blue-black hair bunched between her shoulder and left cheek, her dark blue eyes merry with laughter and the sheer joy of life. But even Nikki, usually so dependable, contributed her share to the general blah of the week. Without any preamble whatsoever, Nikki asked:

"Have you written your Mom? Have you congratulated Dr. Hansen?"

Laura said crossly: "Be a big girl."

"I like your Mom," Nikki said outright. "I guess I like Dr. Hansen, too. Or I would, if he wasn't the dean of Kenyon Junior College. I just know that man will give me a bad time when I go there as a student."

To change the painful subject, Laura asked, "What did Miss Aronstam say when you told her my demotion was unfair?"

Nikki sat up, her face all animated. "Now that's a really interesting thing, Laura. She said that different girls become ladies in different ways. Did you know that she thinks you're spoiled?"

That was so comical that Laura had to laugh.

"Anyway," Nikki said, turning suddenly gloomy, "Miss Aronstam thinks Beverly will be a better unit leader than you. I don't get that, myself. I thought you ran the Deer Fern Unit very well."

Laura shrugged and made her face perfectly unreadable, determined never to let Nikki know that she cared. Then along came Beverly Anglin, her black eyes hopping mad, her cheeks bright red. "Glory smoke, Laura," Beverly cried, "what's gotten into you? You know you're not supposed to take off without permission! I have twenty-five kids waiting for a songfest, and you take off without notice."

For Laura, that was the straw that broke the camel's back. She went icy. She stood up and asked with a deadly calm: "Did you ask me to lead a songfest? I thought you told me to clean up that pigsty you've turned our cabin into. Oink, oink, oink!"

Beverly Anglin drew a deep breath.

Laura, much to her satisfaction, beat Miss Beverly Anglin to the punch.

"Oh," she said sweetly, "don't bother to fire me, Beverly. I've quit. And oink, oink, oink to you."

Blonde head high, her back broomstick straight, Laura went back to the cabin to pack her bags.

From that moment on, she vowed, there would never again be a week that could be added up to a big, soggy blah.

Chapter 4

Laura left Camp Mosher without saying good-bye to anyone. She packed her camp locker while everyone was having dinner, and then she showered and changed into her beige cotton suit and followed one of the back trails to the area near the highway where the camp caretaker lived. She found Mr. Scofield sitting in a green wooden lounge chair under the great eucalyptus tree that was his pride and joy. He took the pipe from his mouth and waved the stem at her genially. "All dressed up for a movie, huh?" he asked. "Well, I guess I can be coaxed to take you to town. I'm running out of pipe tobacco."

"Actually, Mr. Scofield, you shouldn't smoke.

Ask anybody! Ask even Mrs. Scofield!"

He gave her a most queer look but never said a word. He knocked the dottle from his pipe and motioned for her to follow him to the garage. About five minutes later he was driving them along Highway 9 toward Boulder Creek. As usual, he kept the speed down to about twenty miles an hour so that he would miss no sight worth seeing. She broke the silence by saying quickly, "Actually, Mr. Scofield, I'm not going to a movie tonight. Something's come up at home, and I have to talk to Mrs. Gammage."

His whitish brows climbed up his forehead and almost met his whitish hair. "Say," he exclaimed, "you surely don't think I'll drive you clear to Kenyon Junior Colege! That's twenty-two miles each way!"

"I'll gladly pay you."

"Will you, now! And since when do I take the hard-earned money of babies?"

"I'm almost sixteen, you know."

"Closer to fifteen."

Laura did a quick exercise in arithmetic, using

the fingers on both hands. "Well," she confessed, "I guess you're right. But pretty soon I'll be fifteen and a half, and after that I'll be right. Would you make a fibber out of me for just a couple of months?"

"Everybody's in such a hurry to grow up. Why is everybody in such a hurry to grow up? You take a tip from me and don't hurry things. The second you try to hurry nature, you get into trouble."

"Really?"

Mr. Scofield was reminded of a yarn. He told her to fill his pipe for him. Laura did, and wondered as she did so why anyone in his right senses would smoke a tobacco called London Dock. Docks were dirty places. Who wanted to smoke the sweepings of a dock in London? And thinking of London—

Laura changed the mental subject again.

"I hope you won't poison yourself," she said, giving the pipe to Mr. Scofield. "I sincerely hope so."

"Girl lady," he laughed, "there isn't a finer or sweeter tobacco than London Dock. And I don't inhale a pipe. It's just the taste a man's after, see?"

"I honestly think," Laura said, "that I'd rather eat boiled carrots."

"Let me tell you my yarn!"

So he told the yarn while the miles rolled off behind them, while they followed the two-lane, curving road through Boulder Creek and then more forest, through Ben Lomond and then more forest, through Felton and then more forest.

Laura thought it a silly yarn, a typical yarn told by adults to stress a point they could just as easily have made with a few well-chosen sentences.

"Yup," Mr. Scofield said, "you sure get in Dutch when you try to hurry nature. Take when I was your age and full of beans. I thought to myself: I'm a man now, a ring-tailed bobcat sure enough. So I went to a dock in San Francisco, and I hired on as cabin boy on one of them lumber boats that used to ply between ports in California and ports up in Washington and Oregon. Well, girl lady, there come up a storm, a real howler, one of them storms that gives you green seas over your bows like you don't see green seas very often.

Something got stove in, see? All hands had to save the ship, see? The captain he yells for me to help the ship's carpenter rig something over that hole in the keel, see? So down I go, a ring-tailed bobcat sure enough, and we nail a lot of boards together, and then we haul the planks overside and the carpenter he tells me hold them fast if I hope to see another sun fire up that old eastern sky. But that load it got heavier and heavier for a boy who wasn't the man he thought he was. See what happens when you try to hurry nature? Sooner or later you get in a spot you wouldn't have been in if you'd just been content to be what you was. Well, girl lady, that load got heavier and heavier still. All my muscles stood out on my arms like rope. I got the darnedest aches all over me. And that load got heavier and heavier. It slipped! Girl lady, I dug holes in the deck with my heels to keep that load from slipping any more. And the carpenter, he yells out that if that load ever slips, the sea will come through that stove-up keel and drown us all. But sure enough that load kept slipping and slipping and slipping. And then—"

Laura gulped. When she saw Mr. Scofield take one puff and then two puffs and then three puffs at his pipe, she was all but ready to pop out of her skin.

"Then *what*?" she asked. "What happened?"

He turned and looked at her solemnly for two or three seconds. Then, in a doleful voice she knew she would never forget, Mr. Scofield said simply, "I drowned."

The letdown was breathtaking. Another mile, at least, rolled on behind them before Laura felt able to speak. Not to be outdone by him, the whopper teller, she sad quietly, "Oh, brother!"

To her disgust, the laughter he had been waiting for came. The laughter just bubbled out of her and kept bubbling, while her eyes watered and her sides commenced to ache.

"Whopper!" she wheezed. "My, what a whopper!"

He smoked on and he drove on, and presently there were the rooftops of Santa Cruz below them, with a lovely white church spire rising from a little valley and the Pacific Ocean all pink and gold in the distance under a huge pink and gold evening sky. The sight reminded Laura of her manners. "I could buy you a shrimp cocktail on the wharf," she said. "Stagnaro's serves wonderful shrimp cocktails. When I was a little girl, Mom and Dad and I used to come to Santa Cruz and have shrimp cocktails there."

"Well, maybe some other time."

He puffed away furiously at his pipe, creating a regular smoke cloud in the cab of the truck. He cleared his throat five or six times, the way people generally do when they feel they must discuss a delicate subject. He eventually asked, "Girl lady, you want to talk about it? Now let's be square with one another, man to man and all that. No slip of a girl pulls the wool over Scofield's eyes. Why, when Scofield was your age, he was a pretty smart ring-tailed bobcat sure enough. You know what I said to Mrs. Scofield when I heard all the talk about you this afternoon? 'Precious heart and Mrs. Scofield,' I said, 'I have a powerful hunch that pretty Laura Gray will be coming along to beg a ride home from me.' That's just what I said to Mrs. Scofield."

Oddly, Laura was relieved to know that she really had not tricked him into driving her home. For the first time since she had gotten into the truck, she stopped fretting about that.

"There's nothing to discuss," she said cheerily. "I always think it's a foolish person who stays where he really isn't wanted. And don't think for a second I don't know why Miss Aronstam demoted me!"

"Why did she?"

"Because it so happens, Mr. Scofield, that my mother sends the camp a hundred dollars every year, and it burned Miss Aronstam up to think I didn't yell three cheers and a tiger for my mother and Dr. Hansen."

"Hey, there, that don't sound too logical to me. I mean, a hundred dollars isn't a fortune, you know."

"If I hear that word again, I'll simply scream."

"What word?"

"Logical! With Clay Chatham, it's logical this and logical that, and I've had it."

Now they came to the freeway. Broad and smooth, the road carried them by Santa Cruz and then through rolling countryside. Here, with no sharp turns and with no clumps of trees to block his vision, Mr. Scofield could really make time. Mr. Scofield did. For fifteen minutes they rolled on and on at almost sixty miles an hour. Then came the last bend in the road, and the turn into the campus of Kenyon Junior College.

At once, a lump came into Laura's throat. The lovely campus always put that lump there when she returned to it at the end of each summer, for somehow the rich green grass and the nicely spaced maples and sycamores and oaks had about them a serenity she never felt anywhere else except in a church. A notion popped into her mind. "Mr. Scofield," she announced, "I'll walk the rest of the way!"

"When Scofield delivers them, Scofield delivers them."

"Please?"

He studied the thin, lightly freckled, rather lovely wistful face of Laura Gray. A big bear of a man, he could be and was quite gentle. "Sure," he rumbled, "sure. And you be warned by my terrible fate when I was your age. There ain't nothing but drowning ahead for a ring-tailed bobcat that's got more pride than brains."

Laura stood waving until the truck had turned back into the freeway. She went under one of the oaks and took a quick glance around and then took off her nylon stockings and her shoes and stuffed the stockings into her handbag. Loving the feel of the warm, silky grass on her feet and between her toes, she took the short cut across the campus and went up over the moon bridge spanning the ornamental pond the students called Lake Moneygrabber. If you threw a penny into Lake Moneygrabber, she remembered, you were sure to get passing grades. So, at least, the students thought. But according to her mother, it was really impossible to buy passing grades with anything other than careful, systematic study. And according to her mother—

Again, with the skill that comes through practice, Laura changed the mental subject. She had things to do before nightfall, by golly, to make the house livable for the brief time she planned to live there!

Off she went at a run to beat the darkness home.

Chapter 5

It gave Laura Gray a strange feeling to waken at nine o'clock on Sunday morning in her own bed in her own room facing the Pacific Ocean. On this particular day of all the days she would live, she decided, she had become a woman. Definitely! Would she be in this bed in this room if she had not taken control of her life and come there? Obviously not. And did she regret the decision she had made at Camp Mosher the previous afternoon? Ridiculous. Well, there you were. As her Aunt Ruth was always saying, the day you could take control of your destiny and not look back with regret for a lost childhood was the day you became a woman.

Laura settled back on her three pillows and gave serious thought to the day that lay ahead. She would have breakfast, then scrub the last of Camp Mosher from her hide and bones, then go to church in Kenyon. Acording to the testimony of truly great people, it was always wise to get the special blessing of God before you commenced a great undertaking. So be it. Whatever was good enough for truly great people was certainly good enough for Laura Gray! Then, after church, she would get copies of the Sunday newspapers put out by the big newspaper companies in San Francisco and San Jose and Santa Cruz and Kenyon. She would not look through the Help Wanted ads, though, until after lunch, because it was always a mistake for her to try to concentrate on anything major while she was eating. She would bring the papers home and check all the ads and decide which jobs she had a chance of getting and which she would have to pass over. Then, after a swim or maybe just a walk along the beach, she would settle down at her desk and write a flock of letters to the employment people at the different companies whose ads had interested her.

Afterwards?

Laura snapped her thumb and forefinger gaily. Well, time enough to worry about her evening schedule when she had gotten most of the day taken care of!

Hungry, Laura went downstairs to investigate the food situation. It gave her an unpleasant shock to find an empty refrigerator and bare cupboard shelves. She had to sit down and tell her stomach to be patient while she tried to figure out what to do next. She got the solution to the immediate problem in quite a hurry. She went upstairs, got into her tangerine quilted robe and slippers, then scooted across the seven lawns along Faculty Row that separated her mother's residence from the Mc-Clouds'. Three rings of the front-door chimes, and Mrs. McCloud opened up. "Love a monkey!" Mrs. McCloud ejaculated. "I thought I saw lights in your place last night. What blew you in, and why?"

Mrs. McCloud started to reach down to go through the old hug and kiss routine, but in the

nick of time she remembered the pact the Mc-
Clouds and Grays had made. "Well," she said,
covering up, "do come in, by all means. Do you
think that fashion style will sweep the country?
My, how times have changed. When I was your
age, any girl who appeared in her bedroom clothes
was taken back to her bedroom for a paddling."

Laura happily followed Mrs. McCloud and the
good smell of frying bacon to the kitchen. "Not
that I'm at all famished," Laura said tactfully, "but
I could eat something. Naturally, I'll repay you as
soon as I've gotten my supplies in."

"Now, now, it's a wretched friend who can't
give a friend a meal now and then. My goodness,
I'll say that when you Grays decide to surprise
people, you *do* surprise them. Oh, and how's my
Nikki? Not that I care."

"Very well for a girl who has aralia fever."

Mrs. McCloud asked: "*What*? Do you mean to
stand there and tell me that Nikki's *ill*?"

Laura tried not to giggle, but the giggle came
out anyway. "I thought you didn't care, Aunt
Ruth. See what happens when you go against

nature? You drown."

"Oh, dear," Mrs. McCloud said, "I'd just about forgotten what a horror it is to have a teen-ager in the house. Go away. Go grow up or something."

Laura ambled into the living room to chat with Professor McCloud while Aunt Ruth prepared breakfast. She found Professor McCloud following his customary Sunday morning procedure. Seated in his large red leather chair in dressing gown and Ascot scarf, he was reading some portion or other of the *Journal of John Woolman*. For his money, he had once said, the *Journal of John Woolman* was the finest book short of the Bible that anyone could read for guidance in the art of keeping one's spiritual house in order. It always struck Laura as strange that Professor McCloud was so bent upon keeping his spiritual house in order, for the truth was that he never kept his study in order or his workshop in order or even the desk top in his office in the mathematics department of the college. Puzzled by the inconsistency in his behavior, Laura made herself comfortable on the early-American double settee and studied Professor McCloud while he studied his book. Abruptly, he smiled. "Here's a good line," he said. "Quote. The more fully our lives are conformable to the will of God, the better it is for us. Unquote."

He closed the book. "Did I ever tell you," he asked, "that in 1742 Mr. John Woolman, who was then working as a clerk in New Jersey, flatly refused for religious reasons to make out a bill of sale for the purchase of a Negro woman? From that time on he was a dedicated foe of slavery, and many historians claim that no small part of the enthusiasm for the general emancipation movement that later swept this country is traceable to Mr. Woolman's work."

"I tried reading him twice," Laura reported. "I hate to tell you this, Uncle Rob, but it's a ghastly book. I fell asleep both times."

One of the grand things about Professor McCloud was that he never became annoyed if you disagreed with something he believed or said. "To each his own," he said, grinning. "Would you care to talk now or after breakfast?"

"Talk?"

"I had a telephone call around midnight. Miss Aronstam. She was concerned because you left Camp Mosher in a huff. Girls in a huff, she informed me, frequently do scatty things. So she wanted to know if you had indeed come home."

"After breakfast would be better, I think, Uncle Rob. Not that there's anything major to discuss."

"As you wish. Perhaps I ought to tell you, however, that I had a telephone call from Nikki this morning."

"The trouble with too many people, it seems to me, is that they worry about a friend when they really don't have to. I mean, I'm practically sixteen, after all. I'm pretty tall for my age and awfully strong. Also, I've been a straight-A student through high school so far, which means I'm not absolutely a mental clinker. So all right! Lots of people don't start out with half the advantages I have."

"Oh, is that what you're doing? Starting out, striking off on your own?"

"Well, why not? I mean, there's a great big

exciting world out there, Uncle Rob. Lots of things to do, lots of people to meet, lots of things to see."

Mrs. McCloud came in with two glasses of orange juice on a tray. She sat down beside Laura in a companionable way and said with slushy sentimentality, "I really didn't mean what I said about teenagers in the house. I miss my Nikki, in fact. How's she getting along at the camp?"

"Very well, Aunt Ruth. Miss Aronstam put Nikki on her staff, which is always a good sign. If she thinks you have the makings of a unit leader, she sticks you on her staff awhile so that you can get a broader picture of the whole camp's operation."

The McClouds looked at one another so proudly they were cute. A girl, Laura thought, was really lucky to know such folks. Professor though he was, Uncle Rob was not an old fuddy-duddy, and as for Aunt Ruth—well, Aunt Ruth was the liveliest and most fun-loving person of thirty-eight whom you could hope to meet.

A sudden memory sent a shiver of pain through

Laura.

Professor McCloud demonstrated to her once again that, if he was not psychic, he was pretty close to being so. "You mustn't brood over the past," he told her gently. "It's never particularly adult to think this or that event shouldn't have happened or to let the fact that it did happen blight your life. As I often tell Nikki, a girl in her middle teens is getting too close to womanhood to behave or to think in a juvenile fashion."

"I was thinking about Dad, Uncle Rob. I guess if Dad hadn't drowned in the ocean, he'd be pretty much like you, wouldn't he? He wouldn't be an old fuddy-duddy, either."

Mrs. McCloud said energetically, "I have too much to do today to wait around for people to finish their juice. I don't know what you people plan to do, but I plan to get breakfast down the hatch."

By this time, Laura was far too hungry to worry overly much about her manners. She jumped up and led the way to the dining nook in the kitchen. "Just keep track of what I eat," she told Mrs. McCloud, "and then I'll pay you back after I've shopped."

"Oh, we'll do that, all right. We're just poor people trying to make ends meet."

It was a good breakfast and it was a fun breakfast. Professor McCloud announced that he had plans for a most active summer, plans that included a visit to the Grand Canyon. And the trip, he informed his wife, would be a camping trip. They would rough it all the way. At once, Mrs. McCloud said that if he wanted to rough it, he would have to rough it alone. "I'm a weak city girl," she teased, "remember?" And this, of course, made Professor McCloud all but swagger in his chair. "Oh," he bragged, "I come from rugged stock, all right. Laura, did I ever tell you that my grandfather crossed the plains in a covered wagon?"

Next, Professor McCloud told them ridiculous stories about his grandfather's adventures during the plains crossing. With his blue-gray eyes sparkling and his handsome face looking astonishingly youthful, he fascinated Laura so utterly she had to be reminded two or three times to go on with her breakfast. A sudden thought popped into Laura's mind. If her mother had married a man like Professor McCloud, she thought, then it would have been all right. But to have married a drip like Dr. Hansen, the icy dean of Kenyon Junior College! What a ghastly thing to have done! Why, it was practically a desecration of her father's memory, because her father had been a warm-hearted and laughing man, just like his good friend Professor McCloud!

Laura volunteered to do the dishes after breakfast, but her scheme did not work. "We'll have our talk now," Professor McCloud said grimly; and he led her along the hall to that study of his he never could keep in order. He took a stack of mathematics journals off the seat of the chair near the desk and nodded for her to sit down. Then, behind his desk, he said joltingly, "I think I'm ashamed of you, Laura. Look at you! It won't be too long before you're indeed a woman, yet you behave like a child under ten. Everything must be as you want it to be, or you won't play. People must do as you wish, or your feelings will be bruised and you'll run away. I was very disappointed in you when Miss Aronstam telephoned last evening. I came very close to telling my wife not to let you in when you rang this morning. What in the world do you think you're doing?"

"Sir, I—"

"No. You've done too much thinking and too much talking about your imagined woes and problems. Your father died on your seventh birthday. Now you're well over fifteen, and too many years have gone by for you to have a perfectly clear memory of your father. Your basic trouble can be summed up in one word: selfishness. You want your mother all to yourself. You want to be the one and only creature in your mother's life. Now I know the reason for that, of course. Having lost one parent, you're basically frightened by the thought of losing your other parent. But it's still a selfish thought. You give no thought whatsoever to your mother's needs or your mother's happiness."

"Sir, I—"

"It won't work," he interrupted. "Your mother is married to Dr. Glenn Hansen now, and regardless of what you do, that marriage will last. If you thought that by quitting your job and coming here you'd compel your mother to return home, you're due for a disappointment. Your mother anticipated you would do something like this, and she left sufficient money for you at the bank to support you until she does come home."

Laura was dumbfounded. "Mom *anticipated* that I'd quit?"

"Laura, it never was a secret to your mother that you wanted to keep her all to yourself. So of course she realized that a person who's childish in one way is rather apt to be childish in another way."

"That's insulting! Mom had no right to think such insulting things about me!"

"Well, that's neither here nor there. Do you return to the camp or remain here? Do you write a letter of congratulations to Dr. Hansen, or do you sulk?"

"Mom sneaked away to marry him! She never once told me!"

"Oh, that isn't true, you know. Your mother did her best to tell you before you went off to camp a couple of weeks ago. But you wouldn't let her talk, would you?"

Laura stared, wondering how in the world Professor McCloud had learned so much about her.

Then, suddenly bored with being scolded, Laura excused herself in a hurry and went back to her bedroom.

Chapter 6

As it turned out, Laura never did get a chance to shop for food or to pay Mrs. McCloud back that Sunday. When she reached Kenyon after a two-mile walk, she was warm enough and thirsty enough to crave two chocolate bombshells at Milburns. Sitting at one of the marble-topped tables was Keith Moller, eating a pineapple sundae. Big, black-haired, blue-eyed Keith saw her almost as soon as she saw him, and he stood up and smiled and beckoned before she could execute a strategic retreat. "You should always wear blue," Keith said. "You and blue get along pretty well."

Laura sat down, feeling she had to. She wished, however, that Keith would be more sparing with his compliments. He was a nice boy, all right. Riding with him in a car definitely was not like riding with an ardent octopus. You were never taken by surprise, when you were with Keith, by an arm that zipped around you all of a sudden to snuggle you close. But just the same, she did not like all those compliments. A girl did not have to be a big brain to figure out that a boy who complimented her endlessly was becoming enchanted by her magic. The last thing in the world she wanted at this stage in her development was an enchanted steady. An enchanted steady could be a dreadful problem, according to some of the girls she knew, and she had sufficient problems as things were.

"I didn't mean to embarrass you," Keith said, misunderstanding her silence. "Things just pop out, that's all."

Laura made a great effort to look him over coolly. Next she asked: "Should they just pop out, though? According to what I've heard, silence is still equivalent to gold."

Keith came down on his chair with a force that made the chair squeak. "I'm one person you can't ever argue with," he said cheerfully. "What will you have?"

"A chocolate bombshell, I guess."

Keith went over to the counter and ordered the bombshell and stood waiting for it to be concocted. He was really quite handsome, Laura suddenly noticed. He still had some growing and filling out to do, but already he was at least five feet ten inches tall and weighed around a hundred and fifty pounds or so. He would be a really bruising fullback on the Kenyon High football team this autumn, and if he kept on growing he would eventually develop into quite a hunk of man.

Still, Laura thought firmly, she was not interested in anything except a casual relationship with Keith Moller.

After he had served the chocolate bombshell, he sat studying her with twinkling eyes. "What do you want to know?" he asked.

"Nothing," Laura fibbed.

"You're a peculiar girl," he notified her. "At the camp you always insist that the kids behave well and speak nothing but the truth and do what-

ever they can to help each other. But your behavior pattern is pretty different. Take now. For
your information, curiosity is all but bugging your
eyeballs."

"I made a decision," Laura told him flatly, "and
that's that."

"Well, Beverly Anglin flipped when she realized you'd left. The first thing she told me is that
if you think she'll send your camp locker and suitcases to you, you have another thing coming. She
said she never could stand sneaks."

"Sneaks?"

"Well, you never did submit a resignation in
writing, you know. And you never officially told
Beverly that you were leaving. So she was left high
and dry, sort of, when you sneaked off like that."

Laura felt her cheeks become hot. She tried to
say it all depended upon a person's point of view,
but the words stuck in her throat. Clearly, she had
left Beverly high and dry in the Deer Fern Unit,
even though she had not deliberately planned it
that way.

"Anyway," Keith said, "Miss Aronstam told

Beverly to cool off, because you'll be back at work on Monday."

Laura pushed the bombshell away from her, too flabbergasted to enjoy it. "Miss Aronstam should live so long!" she flared. "My demotion was utterly unfair, Keith. All right; I admit that I did goof at the swimming pool. I shouldn't have let that redheaded boy play. But think of it another way. If a unit leader always ruled with an iron hand, most of those kids would never have fun. What I'm saying, I guess, is that hindsight makes everybody wise. If the boy hadn't punched Derinda, though, no one would have said I goofed when I allowed him to remain in the pool and play basketball."

"Did you tell Miss Aronstam that?"

"I never had the chance. She was cross and upset. She started to romp all over me the moment I entered her office. I admitted I hadn't been thinking, and I said I suppose I had assumed the boy would settle down and behave. But that's all, really, I ever had the chance to say. Miss Aronstam said she would accept no excuses or pointless apologies, and demoted me just like that."

"Wow."

Laura sighed. "In all fairness to Miss Aronstam," she went on, "I have to admit she was given a shock. I guess when you're responsible for so many crippled children, you get a lot of tension inside you that has to be worked out of your system one way or another. But Camp Mosher is definitely behind me. I plan to get a full-time paid job and maybe live in San Francisco or San Jose."

"I'll bet on Miss Aronstam."

Laura sniffed eloquently and then finished her bombshell. When they were back outdoors, Keith said that he would like a closer look at the ocean, so they walked crosstown to Municipal Beach, and Laura took her shoes and socks off, and they went down to the hard-packed sand along the water's edge. Here and there were great mounds of seaweed left by the day's high tide. Little clouds of fleas hovered over each mound, and in among the brown-gold tentacles Laura spotted some sand crabs. "Darned good bait," she told Keith. "When my father and I came here to surf-fish, it was always my job to find bait. I was what Professor McCloud used to call a little mouse, but I could always find bait one way or other."

Laura stopped short. Creamy surf surged in, and Keith caled a warning, but her practiced eye told her the water would never reach her. It gave her a strange sensation to think that somewhere out under all that sparkling blue water, her father had found his final resting place.

"Nikki told me about your mother and Dr. Hansen," Keith said. "He's a nice fellow, Dr. Hansen. A couple of years ago my father was having it rough, and I told Dr. Hansen about it while I was delivering his Sunday paper. Dr. Hansen telephoned someone at the Bank of America, and my father was called in for an interview, and he's been with the bank ever since."

"Really?"

"You can hate me if you want to, Laura, but you've got the wrong slant. You have a wonderful mother, even if she does teach English. She wouldn't do anything to hurt you. Any person could tell that just by watching her when she's watching you."

Laura was intrigued. "How does she watch me?"

Keith picked up a pebble and tried to skip it across the water. He got two skips, but a roller came in and broke over the pebble before it could skip a third time. Keith said, "She watches you like a person who doesn't believe her good luck."

A wonderful warm, tingly feeling ran through Laura.

"Frankly," Keith said, "you're having some good luck, too. My guess is that if you meet him halfway, Dr. Hansen will be a pretty good Joe to have around the house."

"Keith, it's just that—"

"Look, Laura, don't ever kid yourself that you're so selfish you'll cheerfully blast your mother's happiness into smithereens. You might blast, sure, but you'd have a guilty conscience all your life. And do you know why? Because you're the sort of girl who'll actually carry a crippled kid a mile on her back to show that kid a deer and its fawns in the woods. I've seen you do that; don't think I haven't. So don't try to kid me you're one of those hard-boiled blondes who thinks only about herself."

"I'm *not* trying to blast her happiness. I'm just trying to work out my own destiny."

"Whether you're trying to or not, Laura, you'll blast it all right if you leave home because of Dr. Hansen. After that, you won't love yourself. You know what I think?"

"I'm not sure I want to hear."

"I think you ought to give your mother the same chance at happiness that you gave that crippled girl I saw you carrying to see the deer and the fawns."

Brother, Laura thought, did Keith Moller have an educated tongue that could twist things and confuse you!

"In other words," Keith said, "why don't you be a good sport, Laura, and give your mother and Dr. Hansen and Rose Davis and others a break?"

"And who's Rose Davis, please tell?"

"That's the blind girl Miss Aronstam says you'll be helping commencing tomorrow. Some challenge, huh?"

"I am *not* returning to Camp Mosher, and that's definite!"

But Keith just smiled. They finished their walk, and then he surprised her with a dinner invitation and he drove her home to the campus to shower and change. He arranged to pick her up at five o'clock sharp, and off he drove, whistling, so geared up because she had given him a date that he was comical. A peculiar thing happened as Laura waved from the stoop. Through her went the oddest conviction that in many ways she was more mature emotionally than Keith and that for that reason she had to look after him just as she used to look after the kids in the Deer Fern Unit. But all that faded from her mind when she stepped into the living room to find Miss Aronstam waiting for her. Somehow, the expression on Miss Aronstam's face made her feel terribly young and gauche.

"Professor McCloud let me in," Miss Aronstam explained. "He thought that if you saw me waiting outdoors, you might perhaps avoid this meeting. I told him I've never had cause to doubt your courage, but he seemed to think it best I wait here for you."

It occurred to Laura that she was the hostess, and she asked, "Would you like some tea or coffee, Miss Aronstam? I could get some next door. I haven't done any shopping yet."

"Laura, you and I know one another fairly well by this time. I could take two hours or five hours to say what I've come to say. On the other hand, I can say it all in just a minute or so. I'll choose the quick approach. I think you know there's a right way and a wrong way to do anything. I think you know that when a person of principle agrees to assume certain obligations, he discharges those obligations regardless of the pressures to which he may be subjected. I think you know that your flight from camp was and is inexcusable. Last night I decided to have your belongings sent to you. I'm too busy with the crippled children to baby you. But then, upon thinking things over, it occurred to me that I was much too harsh on you the evening after that incident at the pool. Very

well. You may return to Camp Mosher. Not as a
unit head, please understand, because it wasn't the
demotion that was harsh but merely the way I
announced it to you."

Laura sat down and wondered why on earth
Miss Aronstam imagined for a moment that she
wanted to return to Camp Mosher. Before she
could ask that question, however, Miss Aronstam
said, "Be a big girl, dear. Your mother's marriage
begins a grand new experience for you. And your
new work at the camp—well, it will be a challenge. I'm not sure anyone but you can handle the
challenge, and—"

"I'd rather not, Miss Aronstam."

"Nonsense. You wouldn't want me to send
Rose Davis away, would you? I know you better
than that."

"You'd send her away?"

"I'd have to, dear."

Laura all but ground her teeth with helpless
fury. This was a darned unfair method Miss Aronstam was using to force her to go back. And yet—

Laura sighed.

Miss Aronstam read acceptance into that sigh. Up she hopped, as peppery as ever. "Splendid," she said. "And now that you've accepted, let me tell you something I couldn't say before for fear you would think I was flattering you for an ulterior purpose. I have always considered you my most promising helper at the camp. That's why I was so harsh with you. I expect more from you than from others."

Deeply stirred, Laura led her to the door.

Chapter 7

It was arranged that Laura should drive back to Camp Mosher after her dinner date with Keith Moller. Keith was completely unsurprised when he was told the news. "Why do you think I invited you to dinner?" he asked. "I wanted to celebrate your return to common sense!"

Keith took her to dinner at Scopazzi's in Boulder Creek. The main dining room was crowded, but a table was found for them at one of the windows overlooking the side parking lot. Although there was all the light anyone needed for eating purposes, Keith asked their waitress to light the table candle for them. The waitress, a plump, pleasant woman, looked at their faces in the faint candle glow and said that she had never seen a more attractive couple anywhere. Keith was hugely pleased, the goop. "Ma'am," Keith said with impressive poise, "I agree with you a hundred percent."

Keith, who had been there before, urged Laura to forget the menu and try the chicken cacciatore. Something about the big-deal posture of Keith on his chair warned Laura to open the menu, and she all but flipped when she saw that the de luxe dinner Keith wanted her to order cost three dollars and fifty cents. "Come easy, go easy," she scolded. "Really! The very idea!"

"But this is our first dinner together."

"And it'll be the last, Keith Moller, if you throw your money around that way. If there's one thing I can't stand, it's a person who'll work hard all week just to get some money and then throw it away that way. Anyway, what about your college education? If money means so little to you, why don't you give it to your folks to save for you until you need it for college?"

"I didn't know I was going to college."

Laura reserved that topic for later discussion. She looked carefully through the menu and presently decided that a bowl of minestrone soup and a plate of meat balls and spaghetti would prevent her from starving away into nothingness until breakfast tomorrow at the camp. She gave Keith her order and laid the menu down to forestall any and all arguments. "This is the first time I've been here," she told Keith. She hesitated. Then, dismayed to think the public scolding might have offended him, she blurted out, gauche though she knew it was, "As a matter of fact, Keith, this is the first dinner date I've ever had."

Delight a boy and see him bust out with smiles and swagger!

"I'm honored," Keith said. He laid the menu down, too. "I'd like to say," he said huskily, "that I'm honored."

His face was so well-scrubbed and red it reflected the candlelight, especially up around his high, noble forehead. Laura had to shift her gaze from his face, because she knew that if she did not she would sooner or later giggle at his blushes and embarrassment.

There was a long, awkward silence.

Laura wondered fretfully if it was a woman's place to end long, awkward silences. She knew that at the McClouds' home it was Aunt Ruth who usually said just the right thing at dinner parties to get everyone chatting and laughing and relaxed enough in their chairs to eat tons without risking indigestion. Well, she posed the question, what words did you speak if it was your place to end a long, awkward silence? She waited patiently for her mind to answer that question. Her mind let her down. Disgustingly, her mind went blank.

"Bread?" Keith asked. "I never get tired of the bread here."

"No, thanks."

"Weight problem?"

"No."

"How much do you weigh?"

Laura, astonished, asked without a second thought: "Do you just move in and take over and hit the line hard and all that?"

"Well, that's better."

"What's better?"

"Your tongue's wagging again. For a second there you looked as if you were holding a lemon in your mouth and didn't know whether to swallow it or spit it out."

Laura had to laugh. "I did not," she said "You're making that up."

"Always be yourself," Keith advised. "That's what my mother always tells me. I like to hear you talk You have a very musical voice, did you know?"

"Really?"

"Yup. I'm always surprised you've never gone out for glee club."

Laura thought that over, beginning to lose her stiff posture at the table. Although she was totally unaware of it, the candle glow complemented perfectly the clean, wholesome attractiveness of her young face, adding enchanting shadows about her cheekbones and luster to her blue-gray eyes. Wearing her second blue dress of the day because Keith liked blue, every curl of her golden head catching and holding the candlelight, her teeth gleaming,

Laura, in turn, complemented both the candle glow and the occasion. "I've just never thought I could sing," she told Keith finally. "Mom says that's probably because I can't sing. Mom says that people usually gravitate toward whatever they can do well. Some people gravitate toward singing and others toward teaching and others toward painting. That sounds logical to me, Keith. For instance, how come you decided to go out for football?"

"I just thought I'd like to play."

"Exactly. But what really put that thought into your mind?"

"Gravity?" he teased.

Fortunately the waitress came with their soup. Another second, Laura thought, and she might have kicked the shins of Mr. Keith Moller under the table!

For a first dinner date, the soup was absolutely perfect. Keith insisted that Laura sprinkle cheese liberally over it, and Laura did and found that the cheese added a nice tang to the soup's basic flavor. The spaghetti and meat balls were wonderful, too;

everything nice and garlicky. Twice Laura had to stop and rest before she could eat on, and the second time she rested the waitress came over and asked, "Perhaps you would like your coffee now, miss?"

Miss!

Keith said with that beautiful poise of his, "Coffee for two, if you please."

All of a sudden that was just too much for the natural imp in herself that Laura had bottled up so long. She chuckled and shook her head. "Milk for growing America," she told the waitress. "Keith, you behave now!"

Keith did, too!

When they got back into Keith's Ford, Laura was so well fed and so relaxed she cared not a hoot where they went next or what they did. After she had gotten arranged on the front seat, Keith did a very thoughtful thing. He got a cushion from the rear and tucked it between her head and the seat back and the door frame. "You've had a long, long day, haven't you?" Keith asked. "I know how beat you feel. I feel that way all during the first week of football practice. Want to go to the camp right away or just drive around? It makes no difference to me."

"You're awfully nice, Keith. I mean that."

"Not always. In fact, you'd be surprised. But the way I figure it, you're really very nice to those kids, and somebody ought to be as nice to you. I was joking back at Scopazzi's. I'm going to college. In fact, I'm going to medical school. I'm not going to be a surgeon, you understand. I'm going to be a physician, an internist, as they call it."

"Glory be!"

"There's much about me you don't know, Laura. Why should you? Did you ever know, for example, that I used to be envious of you, really resentful of you?"

"What? How could anyone be resentful of little old me?"

"You don't know this, Laura, but when I first began to deliver newspapers to Faculty Row, I used to look at that beautiful brick house you live in and feel very resentful because you seemed to have all the luck."

"The idea!"

Keith laughed at the child he had been, as if it had all been at least a hundred years ago.

"You grow up in strange ways," he said. "I read that in some book. Some people can grow up in five minutes, and some people can't grow up in a whole lifetime. Would you like to know when I grew up?"

"Are you grown up?"

"Dr. Hansen thinks I'm grown up in the most important way."

Laura was genuinely interested now. She found it no trouble to get her eyes open and to keep them open. She saw that they were moving along Highway 9, probably back to Camp Mosher. But it was all right now, she decided. The wonderful dinner and talk with Keith had done her worlds of good. No matter how many hateful things Beverly Anglin and others might say to her that evening and tomorrow and all summer, they could never take away from her the memory of her first dinner date.

"In what very important way are you grown

up?" she asked, her voice teasing.

"Nothing scares me, Laura. A lot of things used to. Then one day I saw a man hit and killed by a car in Santa Cruz. An odd thing happened inside me. I looked around and felt awfully lucky to be alive, and ever since I've not been afraid of anything."

"That is strange."

"Laura?"

"Keith?"

"The reason I mentioned that is that Miss Aronstam seems to think you're afraid you'll lose your mother to Dr. Hansen. Don't be afraid, Laura. You're smart and beautiful and kind to crippled kids and pretty popular wherevere you are. You'll do all right."

"Do I strike you as being very selfish, Keith?"

"Nope."

"Yet I must be, Keith. After Uncle Rob scolded me this morning, I got to thinking about myself as objectively as I could. I had to concede to myself that basically I really don't want anybody in our house except Mom and me. We've always had such fun together, you see. Keith, I'm awfully mixed up. Do you see? That's my problem, Keith. Keith, why did you bring that up? This has been the loveliest evening of my life, and now I'm going to cry."

"If you shed so much as one dewdrop when you report to Beverly Anglin, I'll cross you off the list."

"*Wheeee!*"

Naturally, however, Laura was not shedding tears when she reported to Beverly Anglin. Along about then she was beginning to realize how very fortunate she was to have kind, well-behaved, level-headed Keith Moller for a good friend.

Chapter 8

Laura was realistic enough to expect to be received most coolly by Beverly Anglin, and she was therefore not surprised when Beverly merely nodded to her from the porch of the cabin Laura had left so hotly the evening before. Not anxious to end her grand evening with a spat, Laura went straight into the cabin and put her handbag away in the chest of drawers beside her bunk. Beverly came in and asked, "Have you been told that Nikki McCloud will replace you here?"

"No. It's a good choice that you've made, though. I've found Nikki to be very conscientious and industrious and loyal."

"I'm the sort of girl, Laura, who likes everything to be out in the open. Miss Aronstam asked if I would take you back. I told her I wouldn't if I had any choice. She then asked if I would take Nikki. I said I would. That's how things have been worked out."

"Fine, fine, fine. Do I spend the night here or switch with Nikki now?"

"Oh, tomorrow will be soon enough."

And those were the only words Beverly and Laura exchanged that evening. The next morning, when Keith came along to help Laura with her camp locker and two suitcases, Beverly was out showing Nikki how she expected things to be done in the Deer Fern Unit. Keith grinned and predicted, "Bev will get over her peeve soon enough. Actually, she's a nice girl. Well, where do you move to?"

"Not too far, as a matter of fact. You can't get me out of Division III. According to what Miss Aronstam told me this morning, I'm to move into one of the cabins in Unit 5."

"That's called the Lady Fern Unit now."

"Nice name. I love to see the lady ferns in the

spring. They come up with all those lacy yellow-green fronds. As a matter of fact, I like all ferns."

Miss Humbert came along while Keith was putting the luggage in the hand cart he had trundled along. Miss Humbert greeted Laura with an easy smile and said she was happy to know she would not be losing that ugly face after all. She then took Laura to the big log-style cabin she occupied alone and invited her to have cocoa while they discussed a few important matters. Laura loved the way Miss Humbert had decorated the paneled living room. She was particularly struck by the living-fern pictures Miss Humbert had hung on the wall. Miss Humbert, noticing her approval, took one of the pictures down and laid it on the oblong coffee table. "What you do to make these," Miss Humbert explained, "is to scrounge a piece of pre-shrunk denim and then wash it once more to make certain it won't shrink. Then you trot off to the woods to find an absolutely perfect frond of whatever type of fern you want to display. Next, you place the frond on something flat and then cover it with some cardboard and put little stones here and there on the cardboard to make certain the fern stays flat. I keep the frond under a certain amount of pressure for at least a week. The rest is simple. You tack the denim to the picture frame, and then you stitch the fern frond to the denim. Presto, you have an unusual picture."

"I should think some of the children would like to make such pictures, Miss Humbert. Actually, you could make lovely woodland scenes if you stitched on bits of this and that. For example, the snipped-off end of a bushy young redwood branch could be sewn on and made to look like a tree in miniature."

Miss Humbert nodded. "We'll have to give that a whirl before the summer is over."

After they had sat down to cocoa, Miss Humbert got an organization chart from behind the maple couch and held it balanced on her knees. "Camp Mosher is growing up and changing," she announced. "And there's a place in this organization for you. Now this is what we plan to do over the next two weeks. We plan to change Division I into a wheel chair unit exclusively. As you know, all the cabins in that division were constructed specifically for children in wheel chairs."

"I didn't know that, though!"

"Oh, I thought you did. Well, all the cabins in that division are larger and have unusually wide doorways and special bathrooms designed for convenient use by people who don't get in or out of wheel chairs easily. For example, all the sinks are mounted closer to the floor, and in each toilet booth there are strong hand rails bolted to the walls so the children will have something reliable to cling to while they're getting in and out of their chairs."

Laura was fascinated. "I never guessed how much thought goes into making a camp like this."

"Well, thought has to go into anything, you know. Anyway, Division I will now be a wheel chair unit exclusively. And if you'll look at this chart, you'll see that Division II will now be for the no-sweat crutches cases, children who walk on crutches but who can shift for themselves most of the time. I suppose I'll now hear all you moppet wranglers calling duty in Division II a 'no-sweat duty.' But don't get your hopes up. In the future, only new moppet wranglers will work in Division II. We'll use Division II for training purposes."

Next, Miss Humbert came to Division III, the division Laura had always served in. Division III, it turned out, would be a rugged division, because to it would be sent all problem cases. Laura saw on the chart that the Deer Fern Unit was reserved for problem wheel chair cases, that the Pyracantha Unit was reserved for problem crutches cases, and that other units were reserved for problem cases with bad backs, problem cases with amputations, and so forth.

She looked up quickly at Miss Humbert. "It seems to me, ma'am," she said, "that you're getting all the headaches."

Miss Humbert smiled. "Well, yes and no. Next week I expect to be sharing my cabin here with a full-time nurse. Also, I'll have more moppet wranglers at my disposal. Well, let's get down to specifics, shall we? For the next three weeks you're to be attached to Miss Aronstam's staff to assist in all this reorganization. That will carry us to August, when Rose Davis will be brought here for a month-long vacation."

"A whole month?" That was sensational news to a girl who was beginning her third year at Camp Mosher. "I thought we never took patients for longer than two weeks, Miss Humbert."

A very wonderful glow suddenly lit Miss Humbert's face. "Well," she said, "and this is confidential, please, Camp Mosher has found several extremely generous friends. As you know, this camp is supported by the Friends of the crippled Children League. That's why no charge is ever made for the time a child is here. Well, young lady, one of our new friends suggested to Miss Aronstam that we broaden our scope and include a unit for blind children. Interesting?"

The practical streak inside Laura made her give a guarded answer. "It could be awfully interesting but a lot of work, Miss Humbert."

"But if you love to work with the handicapped, dear, it really isn't work. I can think of nothing finer than to help handicapped children develop into adults who are perfectly able, for the most part, to take care of themselves. One of the new friends of our camp read an article I wrote for one of our university journals. This friend has given the camp a hundred thousand dollars to be used as Miss Aronstam thinks best to develop a camp program for blind children."

Laura had to laugh. "Glory," she said, "you don't need any money like that to develop a camp program for anybody. If Rose Davis doesn't have a good time while she's here, just bend me over and kick me where I stick up highest."

Miss Humbert chuckled. "It's really a bit more complicated," she said, "than giving a child a good time, Laura. The main objective of a camp such as this is to give each child a useful good time. Why do you suppose the crutches division is located farthest from the mess hall and recreation hall and swimming pool? Because we *want* those children to walk long distances every day. The more they walk, the stronger their legs and muscles become, and the more sure-footed they become. Catch?"

Laura made a catching gesture with her hands.

"All right," Miss Humbert said in a tone of decision. "You know what our camp organization is to be, and you know the immediate recreation and rehabilitation problem confronting me. I expect you to draw up a complete camp program for Rose Davis during the next three weeks."

"But—"

Miss Humbert turned around and dropped her crisp, formal manner. "Now let me say one personal thing to you, Laura, as woman to woman. I selected you for this responsibility for three reasons. First, I selected you because you're always willing to work all-out to help the children have fun. Second, I selected you because you're always so patient with the children. For instance, you might have hauled that redheaded boy out of the pool last week had you been the impatient sort. Instead, you gave him every chance to settle down and have useful fun. I've already defended you on that matter to Miss Aronstam. Had I been at the pool, I would have done exactly as you did."

Laura tried to thank her, but Miss Humbert made a charming moue and put her hand over

Laura's mouth."

"And the third reason I selected you," Miss Humbert concluded, "is that you have a grand imagination. You must use that imagination in this assignment. Try to imagine what it's like to be totally blind and all alone in the midst of strangers. Also, try to imagine what it must be like to be sightless in an environment that's strange to you."

The words brought Laura face to face with the enormity of the assignment Miss Humbert had personally selected her for. At once she was filled with all sorts of misgivings, the paramount one being a fear that she did not have it in her to measure up. And then there popped into her mind the statement Keith had made yesterday while he had driven her to Camp Mosher from Scopazzi's. "I looked around," Keith had said, "and felt awfully lucky to be alive, and ever since I've not been afraid of anything."

Laura looked around. She looked at the cozy living room, and she looked at beautiful Miss Humbert, who had so much faith in her, and she looked out one of the windows at the red-barked, green-needled sapling redwood trees ringing the stump of the great mother redwood tree from which they had sprung. And there was a stellar jay, and she could hear a junco, too, and up, up, up through the needled boughs she could see brilliant blue sky and a cottony cloud. To be able to see all these things, she reflected, was really a great privilege. So you were lucky, all right, to be alive; and if you had life, what was there ever to fear?

Laura breathed a deep breath. Without any real fear but perhaps with nervousness in her voice, she said, "Can do, will do, Miss Humbert."

"Grand. You have an hour in which to get settled in your new quarters. It'll be a lonely place for you until Rose comes, but I'm sure you're not afraid of loneliness or the dark or mysterious things that go bomp in the night."

"I'm afraid of nothing, I guess. Isn't that remarkable? I guess Keith taught me that."

Playfully, Miss Humbert tousled Laura's hair. "I'll believe that, moppet wrangler, when you demonstrate you have the courage to write your new father a congratulatory letter."

Laura was puzzled. She tried to figure out just how courage was involved in *that*. Unsuccessful, she asked the question outright.

"Simple," Miss Humbert explained. "A kind of courage is involved in stepping aside for someone else, in subordinating one's own desires for happiness to the desires of someone else. It isn't an easy thing to do. And only the courageous try the more difficult things, catch?"

"Can do, will do!"

"Whoa! That's a rousing statement, all right, but you must never make a personal philosophy out of a statement until you're sure you know what the statement means. And the way you popped that statement out inclines me to believe you're making it an expression of a personal philosophy."

Chuckling, Laura got up from the couch. "With respect," she said, "let me tell *you* something, Miss Humbert. A person can do just about anything he really wills. Mom taught me that a long time ago."

"So?" Miss Humbert challenged.

Never able to resist a challenge, Laura hustled off to write that congratulatory letter.

Chapter 9

The three weeks that elapsed before Rose Davis came to Camp Mosher for Crippled Children were among the busiest, most instructive and most interesting weeks Laura Gray had experienced in all her fifteen and a half years of life. The quality of those three weeks was presaged, really, the second night Laura spent alone in her cabin in the Lady Fern Unit. Naturally, Laura did not know that at the time.

Just after she had finished her scissor exercises to keep her legs sleek and lovely, Laura heard a scratching hound under the floor of the cabin. Her first thought was that it might be a king snake getting himself comfortably settled down for the night. "Have a happy snooze," she called, "but *please* don't waken me early." The scratching sound stopped. Laura got into her bunk and switched off the bedside lamp. She was quite pleased to think that a king snake was living in her unit. If you had a king snake around, you had no reason to fear the presence of rattlesnakes in the vicinity. King snakes were plain death on rattlesnakes. Immune to a rattlesnake's poison, a big old king snake had what it took to constrict a rattler practically into gooey jelly. Hurrah! One less thing to fret about when Rose Davis came to camp.

The scratching sound came again, not from under the cabin this time, but around back. Next, there was a faint thumping sound, then a sound of metal banging on metal, then an awful clanging clash.

Laura got the back light on and the back door open in a hurry. A big raccoon whirled around from the overturned garbage can. Ah, but he was a brave and sassy fellow. First he sat up on his haunches and made begging gestures with his tiny, handlike forepaws. With a strip of white fur across his face and his eyes gleaming and those hands of his going up and down beggingly, he was too cute to be refused alms. Laura went into the kitchen and got some of the bread she had been planning to set out the next morning for the stellar jays and juncos. When she turned around, there was the raccoon in the kitchen with her. Startled, she dropped some of the bread. The raccoon picked up three pieces and then returned to the night. Laura got the door closed in a hurry. Then, intrigued by the tameness of the raccoon, she went outdoors and sat down on the service stoop and scattered the bread over the ground below and just waited. The raccoon came back four times, moving each time in a perfectly nonchalant way that told her he had no fear of her whatsoever. Maybe, she thought, *he* felt lucky to be alive. The fourth time he came back, she noticed that his forelegs were dripping water, and she wanted to bang her head to punish herself for having forgotten raccoons usually wash their food before they eat it. Laura got a pan of water from the kitchen and set it out. But though she waited for almost an hour, the raccoon did not return that night.

But, by golly, she had been adopted!

And by such a zany creature!

The next night the raccoon would have no bread, thank you. Tough, but there it was. And such a jealous, finicky hunk of hair and claws, too! As Keith came along whistling, the raccoon sprang to the concealment of a mock orange bush. The moment Keith sat down on the service stoop, the raccoon came out of hiding and stood there with head thrust forward, growling.

"Go right ahead and growl," Keith said. "I'll make you into a pie soon enough."

Laura was scandalized. "Keith, you wouldn't *eat* a raccoon, would you?"

"They do down south. A 'coon pie is supposed to be pretty good eating."

Because she thought it and felt that way, Laura said: "Ugh."

Keith stepped down from the service stoop. He stood perfectly still for a few seconds, then thrust his right foot forward. The raccoon stopped growling and twisted his head sideways a bit and looked at Laura as if to ask if *this* was what she expected him to eat. Laura tried to restrain her giggle but failed. Keith took another step forward, then another and another. Then, crooningly, Keith said, "Randy, come here."

The raccoon made all sorts of chirping sounds. The raccoon began to tremble and run around and dart toward the woods and dart back to Keith as if it had no idea of what to do or to expect next.

Keith dropped into a crouch. "Randy," he said crooningly once more, "come here."

It did!

While he scratched the raccoon's ears, Keith said, "You could be sued for alienation of affection or something like that, Laura. We had this guy in a cage behind our cabin, and he got away."

"Well, no wonder! How could anybody have the heart to keep him in a cage?"

"Mr. Scofield found him last February. Randy was bleeding and in pretty bad shape. Well, when the shape-up crew came out here in early June, we decided to shift Randy over to our section, because Mr. Scofield gets too many of the campers popping in on him, and he was afraid they'd stick their fingers in the cage."

"Randy should have his freedom," Laura insisted. "It would be perfectly horrible for him to be cooped up with a forest all around him. His forest, at that!"

Keith picked up the right forepaw. "Seems in good shape," he said after a minute or so. "No argument. Randy's on his own, but I'm afraid you're going to have a steady boarder. You feed him meat scraps. Mrs. Borchard is pretty nice about saving them if you ask her."

So, with Randy in her life apparently for the rest of the summer, Laura found her evenings busy and instructive and interesting during the three-week period she was the only resident in the Lady Fern Unit.

Her days, of course, were equally busy and instructive and interesting. The first day she reported for duty in the administration building,

Miss Aronstam appointed her a committee of one
to check into the practicality of undertaking a
full reorganization of Camp Mosher that summer.
Laura made the mistake usually committed by
people inexperienced in the handling of administrative problems. Five minutes after she had been
given the assignment, she was charging off to
Division I. When she got to the division chief's
cabin, she caught Miss Canby hard at work
teaching a boy on crutches how to climb a flight
of stairs without holding onto a banister. The boy
was plain scared. He had a right to be, in Laura's
opinion. Knowing the boy rather well, she knew
that his right arm sometimes buckled under the
weight he put onto it when he walked. It never
mattered much if his right arm buckled while he
was on the ground. He just retrieved his balance,
and that was that. But how could he possibly re-
trieve his balance while he was up on a narrow
step and had no maneuvering room? And what
if he fell?

Tactfully, Laura got behind the boy so that he
could not see her. Next, she pointed to her right

arm and then to his right arm and shook her head vigorously at Miss Canby. Miss Canby promptly said to the boy, "Time out. Laura, have you business with me? Let's get into the cabin, shall we?"

In the cabin, Laura told Miss Canby about the boy's right arm. Then encouraged by Miss Canby's interest, Laura passed on other information she had gleaned from crutches cases in the past. "Actually," she told Miss Canby, "walking on crutches is a lot trickier than most people realize. Last year we had a boy here who talked about crutch-walking in terms of leverage and sustained momentum and friction balance and things like that. One thing he told me is that you have to be positive at all times that either your feet or your crutch tips are on solid, reliable ground. We got to talking about climbing stairs, and he said too many doctors and nurses think it's important to go up a flight of stairs in as nearly a normal fashion as possible. Then he showed me something I won't ever forget."

"My, how melodramatic!"

Laura wondered if all college girls who specialized in social work also specialized in teasing.

"Miss Canby," she chuckled, "hear this. Most times people don't have stairs to themselves when they go up or down them. And lots of times people are jostled, right?"

"Right."

"Well, then, suppose a boy on crutches is jostled just after he's started to bring his legs up to the next step."

"He grabs the rail."

"How? Both hands are on the crutch handles and are supporting all his weight while he's hoisting his feet up. It would be physically impossible for him to shift all his weight to one hand and grab the rail with the other."

"Time out, you monkey! Big brain has to think."

Laura pulled two armchairs fairly close together and got between them and put a hand on each chair arm to support her weight and then drew her feet up under her. "If I let go of either chair arm," she said, "I'd be down before I could grab anything else."

"But I have seen crippled people go up or down stairs that way."

"I'll bet you'll find they have one good leg. But this boy has both legs in braces and could never balance himself in an emergency if he had to."

"By golly, this is interesting! All right. End of lesson until I chat with Dr. Napier. Now, then, what brought you over here?"

Laura told her about the assignment.

"Fine, fine, fine. What's your plan of attack?"

"My what?"

"What are you checking up on, and why? What standards will this division have to meet? In what way may we improve our services if we huff and puff a bit? That sort of thing."

"Why, I just thought I'd look around, that's all."

Miss Canby laughed. "Now there's a fine amateurish way of doing things, I must say! All right, all right, I'll stop teasing you. Since you gave me a useful tip, I'll return the favor. Get right back to your desk and figure out your plan of attack. Decide what you're looking for, what changes might have to be made here, and so forth. Then when you know what you're after, come here and look us over. Honey bun, I have news for you. Proper administrative work is done with brains, not legs."

Chagrined, Laura went back to the administrative building. She got a writing tablet and a pencil and sat down at her desk near a window. She remembered that Miss Humbert had told her to use her imagination to help Rose Davis and had suggested that she try to imagine what it was like to be blind and what sort of special help she would need if she were blind. So Laura tried to imagine herself a wheel chair camper, and then she tried to think of all the special arrangements a wheel chair camper would need if she were to have a happy experience at Camp Mosher.

Then she got a better idea, did Laura Gray. She went over to Miss Aronstam and requested permission to use a wheel chair.

Mechanically, Miss Aronstam said no. "You ought to know better than to ask," she added.

"I do wish you moppet wranglers would understand that a wheel chair isn't a toy."

Laura explained her idea.

Miss Aronstam arched her grayish brows. "Well," she said dubiously, "I approve the idea, but I don't know that I can trust you to use a chair properly. Oh, very well. But no nonsense now, do you hear?"

Back Laura went to Division I, and she spent the next ten days there, rolling here and there in the wheel chair, making notes of doorways that were too narrow, ramps that were too steep, toilet booths that needed expanding, bunks that needed steadying and paths that needed repaving. But these were all relatively minor problems. The biggest problem for the wheel chair brigade, she discovered, involved the paths that led to the mess hall and the recreation hall. Practically every wheel chair case needed help getting up the grade to those places, and this was a major problem, because moppet wranglers could not always be around to assist when the kids wanted to go or come.

By the end of the ten days Laura had quite a report ready for Miss Aronstam.

Miss Aronstam read it and nodded. "Now," she ordered, "do the difficult part. Come up with detailed solutions to these problems. Oh, and I'll want everything attended to by August the first. As of that date, Division I becomes exclusively a wheel chair division."

Laura gulped. And then, remembering her slogan, she said weakly, "Can do, will do, ma'am."

But how? Laura wondered. How?

Chapter 10

Laura disposed of the minor problems during the next two days with Clay Chatham's help. She deliberately solicited Clay's help as a consequence of a chat she had with Nikki McCloud during a night baseball game between two teams of players on crutches. Just before the game started, Clay came over a bit apprehensively and asked Laura if she were still angry with him. Laura was sincerely hurt. "I certainly thought you knew me better than that," she reproved Clay. "I'm the last person in the world to stay angry for longer than a day or two at most."

"I just wondered," Clay said.

Nikki loosed a heartfelt sigh almost the mo-

ment Clay went down to the playing field to re-
trieve all foul balls hit to the right side of the diamond. "I wish Clay would come pleading to me
that way," Nikki said wistfully. "I keep telling
him how simply beautiful I am, but he just never
notices."

"You don't!"

"Yup."

"You brazen fish!"

Nikki was elaborately unconcerned. "I'll have
you know," she reported, "that some of us girls
got to talking about life in general and romance
in particular last night. We were wondering why
it was that women like Elizabeth Taylor have no
trouble getting all those husbands. And we figured out that Elizabeth Taylor has developed a
pretty potent magic. Well, to develop anything
you have to practice, or maybe brainwash a boy,
I don't know. I don't seem to be having any success brainwashing Clay, though."

"I should hope not! You're beginning to sound
like a hunter."

Nikki's dark blue eyes twinkled. "Call me

Diana the Huntress," she joked. Then her eyes stopped twinkling. "I wish, though, that you'd explain something to me. It's pretty clear to everybody that Keith Moller and you are becoming very, very buddy-buddy. So instead of bothering with beautiful, available me, Clay comes to you, pleading."

Disturbed, Laura asked tautly: "Is that what people are saying about Keith and me? It isn't true, you know, I mean, I like Keith and I guess he likes me, but there's certainly no swoon-moon-June in our relationship. As a matter of fact, it's Randy who brings us together, sort of. And then, of course, Randy leaves and we talk about all sorts of things. Serious talk, like why he wants to be a doctor; like how in the world am I going to solve all my administrative problems by the first of August."

"A word to the wise from an ever-loving friend."

"Pitch."

"If you don't want people to think you and Keith are swoon-moon-June, you'd better start associating with other boys. Miss Humbert's a little worried about you. She said that at our age it's best to go with the group so that we'll broaden our social experience."

The news spoiled the game for Laura, even though it was an exciting contest that was not won by the Noble Knights until the tenth inning. That night, sleepless in her bunk because of what Nikki had said, Laura decided to ask for Clay's help with Division I's problems.

Clay's first important contribution was that old "logical" stuff. After he had looked over Laura's report, he excused himself and came back fifteen minutes later with a tape measure and a length of wood. "This stick," he told her, "is five inches wider than a wheel chair is from hub cap to hub cap. Logical. So now we measure. Logical? Sure it's logical!"

So, measuring, they went from cabin to cabin in Division I. When they had all the measurements neatly typed up, Clay jauntily took Laura by the arm and led her off to Mr. Scofield's place. They found Mr. Scofield trying to repair a doll one of the small girls had broken. He was very glad to have company. He took them into his small office at the rear of the shop, and he sat down and got his pipe going and put on his old-fashioned spectacles and studied the lists of measurements. "Yup," he said, "if you're going to measure anything, put it all in inches or all in feet. Inches are best. No big problems here. If doorways have to be widened, then widen 'em, I say. If these were real houses, that would be work. But with cabins—well, you knock off the lintels and frames and go zip with your electric saw and then stick the framing back on. You do have to buy doors. I don't know any way to stretch a door. When I went to school they didn't teach things like that."

"I've checked with Miss Aronstam, Mr. Scofield. There's plenty of money for doors and wood and stuff."

"We do have a real problem in the bathroom, girl lady. Did you measure from toilet pedestal to toilet pedestal? I can move the walls of each booth; those are just plywood on two-by-four stock. But I can't move the toilets, see?"

"I figured one could be removed from each bathroom, Mr. Scofield. That way, you would gain space in the middle."

Zip went his pencil. "I'll just move the walls in toward the middle toilet and let the toilet stay put. Less expense, and if they ever want to change things again, they won't have to put in new fixtures. Always save money, girl lady. People who throw money away wind up working pretty powerful hard in their old age."

Zip went the pencil again. "Girl lady," Mr. Scofield announced, "I'm the best bunk-bracer you ever saw. I lay that to my sailing days. Never try to hurry nature. Did I ever tell you that?"

"Yes, sir."

"That reminds me of a yarn," Mr. Scofield said.

So they had to sit there while he told a yarn.

Mercifully, this yarn was shorter than most of his were.

"Yup," Mr. Scofield said, "you sure get in Dutch when you try to hurry nature. Now I mind when I was your age and full of beans. I never could just go to bed casual like, see? Show me a bed, and I got so whomped up anxious to snooze I'd just give one of them frisky leaps, sort of, to get to that bunk that much sooner. Wham! Girl lady, I had so many bunks bust under me I got disgusted. And that's how I learned the trick of bracing a bunk. That's what you get by trying to hurry the mysterious forces of nature."

And zip went the pencil. "Ramps I can do, and Clay here can get a load of that cold asphalt mix and fill in the ruts in the paths. Anything else?"

"One more thing, sir. I'd like everything done by the day after tomorrow."

Mr. Scofield took the pipe from his mouth. Mr. Scofield removed his spectacles. Mr. Scofield stood up and went to the doorway of his office. His face became redder and redder and redder, and Laura was sure he would burst at least an artery. Then, in a voice she could barely hear, Mr. Scofield said: "Good afternoon."

Laura got out, but not poor Clay, and it took a long, long time for Laura to get away from the sound of that voice that seemed to thunder louder and louder as Mr. Scofield worked himself up into a real storm.

But, by golly, the minor problems were taken care of within the time period Laura had set. Clay turned out to be so handy with tools that Mr. Scofield made him assistant carpenter. Clay, in turn, got a couple of other boys to see to the paths. At the end of the second day of hard work in Division I, Laura borrowed a wheel chair again and checked to make certain all the improvements had been made satisfactorily.

Victory!

The next day, when Miss Aronstam had officially approved everything, Laura got the courage to ask her for ten dollars so that she could treat all who had helped to dinner at Scopazzi's. Peppery Miss Aronstam said not a word about that until they had returned to the administration building. Sitting down, she smiled, and it seemed to Laura that approval was in that smile. The approval, it turned out, was not imagined.

"You could become a most useful administrator," Miss Aronstam said. "Except for your initial error of charging off without thinking things through, you've done astonishingly well. And it's always an excellent idea to reward people who have done far, far more than they're paid to do. Request for ten dollars granted. What about the major problem, though?"

"I'm stumped."

"What ever happened to 'can do, will do'? I like that approach better."

Laughing, Laura said, "Can do, will do."

And then and there—would she ever forget?— the door opened behind her and a rich contralto voice asked wistfully, "Where's my favorite button nose?"

It seemed to Laura that every nerve in her body sprang tinglingly alive inside her. Once, twice, three times she had to try before she could start breathing again. By the time she had jumped up and swung around, her mother was halfway across the office and coming along fast. Things became mixed up for a while. But after three or four minutes Miss Aronstam said sharply, "I don't know why the sight of one another has brought on all those tears. Personally, I find each of you quite attractive. In any event, ladies, this is hardly the place for emotionalism. Laura, you may take your mother to your cabin. If you wish the rest of the day and tonight off, you may leave whenever you wish."

Outdoors in the warm air and bright sunshine, Laura got a grip on her emotions. She said nervously, "I hope my letter was all right. I didn't know what to say."

"It was a sweet letter, dearest. I was quite proud of you."

"Letters like that—they're difficult to write. Keith helped. But boys—well, to them everything has to be bang, bang, bang."

Hand in hand, they walked to the cabin in the Lady Fern Unit. Mrs. Grace Hansen noticed that all the cabins were empty and asked, "Has there been a plague or something?"

"New assignment, Mom. I'll tell you all about it pretty soon. You look well."

"Thank you, dear."

And of all things, Laura ran out of words!

It was weird.

Sitting in the small living room with Mrs. Dr. Glenn Hansen was like sitting with a person you thought you knew but really did not know at all. The face was certainly familiar enough, with its lovely skin and pixie-like smile and warm gray eyes. Definitely, it was the face of the mother hen! But in those eyes and in the facial expression were qualities never seen before, as if the inner woman had changed so utterly she could be called an entirely different person.

What in the world, Laura wondered, could she say to that inner woman she did not know at all?

Her mother said, misunderstanding: "I hope you won't dislike me too much, dearest. I honestly did try in many ways to tell you about Glenn and me. I dare say I should have tried more diligently. But will you please believe one thing: when I left for Europe I had no intention of marrying Glenn this summer. My plan was to let you have a summer of fun and accomplishment and then to tell you of my decision. I thought—"

"It's done, Mom," Laura interrupted, embarrassed by her mother's embarrassment. "You don't have to explain anything, really you don't."

"Laura, Glenn is a fine person. There's room in your life for Glenn."

"Certainly, Mom. I'm sure of that."

"Laura, we have a complete family now. It's as things should be."

Mechanically, not daring to think, Laura said once more, "Certainly Mom, I'm sure of that."

For the first time she could remember she saw uncertainty come into her mother's eyes, and then a peculiar gleam of fear. The gleam of fear reminded her of the gleam she had seen in a wood rat's eyes when she had accidentally cornered it in the kitchen over in the mess hall.

But this was dreadful, Laura thought. After all, this was the mother hen; this was kith and kin home from Europe. Surely she ought to be as generous and kind to the mother hen as she tried to be to perfect strangers.

Somehow, Laura found words that seemed logical to her.

"I'd love to meet Pop," she said. "Why are we

sitting here? You heard Miss Aronstam. I'm on the town."

The gleam of fear left her mother's eyes.

And that, to Laura, was the most instructive thing of all that happened during the three weeks she worked and planned and waited for her major responsibility to come to Camp Mosher for a month.

Chapter 11

For some reason she could not comprehend, Laura found it less wearing on her nerves and mind to meet her new father. He was strolling through the beautiful gardens of the Dean's Residence when she opened the front gate in the white picket fence to step in and welcome him home from Europe. He was much handsomer than she had remembered, and in the wave he gave her when he spotted her was a youthful and quite gay quality she had not noticed in him before. As she crossed the grass, she wondered if she was expected to kiss him. She supposed she was. For better or worse, he was now kith and kin, too, and she could hardly be as formal and reserved with him as she had always been in the past. Certainly it would be a frosty thing indeed just to take his hand and say, "How do you do, sir; aren't the marigolds lovely?"

Dr. Hansen called, "Hi, there, aren't the marigolds lovely?"

Laura stopped dead in her tracks. She tried desperately not to snicker, but snicker she did.

His brow wrinkling, Dr. Hansen turned to look at the marigolds. "Well," he said gravely, "they may be comical at that. I hadn't noticed, myself, but a man doesn't notice everything, eh?"

"I was trying to think of what to say to you," Laura explained, "and I'd just about decided to say, 'Aren't the marigolds lovely?'"

"Oh," Dr. Hansen said, "you've been nervous, too, eh?" The wrinkles left his brow. He seemed to stand straighter. "Well, you mustn't be nervous, you know. As I tell the students at the opening ceremonies each year, you must never be a fainting robin. Always have confidence in your ability to cope with life on whatever terms life proposes. Furthermore—"

His mouth closed. He shrugged. "But I'm sure you don't want to hear the speech I deliver at the beginning of each school year. Frankly, it's a wretched speech."

"Then why do you make it?" Laura had to ask.

"It's expected of a dean, you know. Part of the job. The trustees would be put out if I simply said hello to the students and let it go at that. It's an interesting thing about trustees. When *they* were young they disliked oratorical exhortations to study hard, be pure, and all that. But now that they're grown, they deem it the duty of the adult to exhort the young."

"I hate windy speeches," Laura told him. "I always think a lot of time and energy would be saved if folks just made their points and closed their mouths."

A spotted towhee came hopping through the garden. It stopped to scratch the earth vigorously under a bridal wreath bush. Without thinking, just trying to make conversation, really, Laura asked: "Will it be all right, do you think, if I put some bird feeders up around here? I've always loved to feed the birds."

"Fine. Naturally, you're supposed to think of this place as your home. I'd like to say, if you don't mind, that it hasn't really been a home during the three years I've been dean. A home needs a woman's touch, I'm afraid, and the racket made by the young."

"It's just that an adult's ears are too sensitive," Laura teased. "The young don't make as much racket as adults think."

He came over to her then and took her lightly by the arm and led her toward the big, slate-roofed house. He asked: "Did you know we have fourteen rooms in this house? Even with three in the family and Mrs. Gammage upstairs, we'll all rattle around a bit."

"Not when I give slumber parties, Pop."

"You—er—give slumber parties?"

"There are seven faculty brats, it seems, and during the school year we give slumber parties twice a month. It's loads of fun."

"Oh, I'm sure of that."

They went into the house. Mrs. Gammage was

dusting in the large, rather gloomy living room. Mrs. Gammage came straight over and gave Laura a kiss on the cheek. "Well, young lady," she said cheerfully, "you look as if all that hard work's agreeing with you. How's the project coming along?"

"Yes and no, Mrs. Gammage. I've got all the minor problems solved, but I'm stuck on the major problem."

Laura's mother came yoo-hooing along the walk, and Mrs. Gammage went to open the door. Dr. Hansen said, "Later on, we'll go upstairs and have you select your room. I suppose I ought to say that I'll try to be considerate and helpful, the very model of a model father. I did appreciate your congratulatory letter more than I can ever tell you, and—"

But Laura's mother came in animatedly. She gave Laura a happy swat on the britches, and then she made like a regular tantalizer inchworming in sultry fashion toward her husband. Laura, who had never seen her mother behave that way, was torn between a desire to laugh and a desire to warn the poor man to evade the tantalizer's clutches. In the end she laughed, because poor Dr. Hansen did evade the clutches by making a mock run behind the protective piano.

"Kids," Grace Hansen said, "I'll buy the dinner. What about San Francisco? I'll tell you what: let's spend a week in San Francisco."

Laura called out hastily: "Whoa! I do have to be at the camp tomorrow, you know."

"Oh, that? Nonsense. We'll write Miss Aronstam a nice letter of resignation. Then we'll all pile into Glenn's station wagon and take off on a trip. I've had a nice honeymoon, but you haven't had a proper vacation, see?"

Laura was thunderstruck.

Dr. Hansen came from behind the piano and said easily, "It's always possible, Grace, that Laura enjoys her work and would dislike having to leave it."

"Partly it's that," Laura told him, "and partly it's because I have an obligation. If everything goes well for this blind girl, then next year Camp Mosher may have a hundred or so blind children come for vacations."

"*Blind* girl?"

Dr. Hansen sat down on one of the three over-stuffed sofas in the big, gloomy room. He leaned forward, resting his hands lightly on his knees. "That sounds like an interesting project."

"It really is, Pop." Laura zipped over and sat down beside him, glad to have a chance to discuss the project with someone outside the camp. "Right now I'm working out a regular camping program for this Rose Davis. And that's tricky stuff. Take last evening. I had Nikki blindfold me and lead me to one of the hiking trails and turn me loose. Well, I found out that's no good. I mean, there isn't enough difference between the footing on the path and the footing around the path to let you judge by feel whether you're still on the path or straying from it."

"Hm."

"We can do one of two or three things, Pop. We can stretch logs along the path, or we can set up ropes for use as guide lines, or we can assign a moppet wrangler to every blind individual or group of blind individuals interested in hiking."

Laura's mother came over and perched lightly on the sofa arm. As of old, her hand strayed out to scratch the small of Laura's back. The scratching distracted Laura and therefore irritated her, but she remembered, somehow, to be kind to this woman she knew but did not know any more.

"I should think," Dr. Hansen said, "that guide ropes would be the cheapest and most practical solution to the problem. If you wanted to change the trail for any reason, it would be easier to shift ropes than logs."

"Nikki and I decided that, too, Pop. Actually, a lot of things will have to be worked out when Rose Davis comes. She'll be a sort of guinea pig, I guess. I plan to watch her closely and to make notes and all that."

Laura's mother said, "Well, of course you couldn't possibly leave a job that important, dear. I'm quite proud of you. Will you become a social worker, do you think?"

"I doubt that, Mom. I'm more interested in administration, actually. To me, this is an administrative project; not a thing for a social worker to handle. Miss Humbert, for instance, is thinking in terms of the individual or individuals who will come. I'm really thinking in terms of the supplies and services and instruction and inspiration the individuals will need."

"What was that major problem you mentioned to Mrs. Gammage?" Dr. Hansen asked.

"The three main paths that lead to the recreation hall and mess hall and swimming-pool area. If you have a lot of wheel chair cases, you have a problem for the moppet wranglers. The children can't roll themselves up those paths easily, and the wranglers can't be around all the time to push the chairs. So I've got to figure out some way to make those paths less steep."

Dr. Hansen thought that over, and then he asked, "Have you ever watched cattle go up a hillside? They seldom go straight up. They zig to the left and then zag to the right. By doing that they lessen the grade they'll have to climb with any one step. Naturally, they take four or five steps to climb the same distance they would climb in one if they went straight up the hill, but there's much less strain involved."

"Really?"

"It's an interesting thing about straight lines and curves, Laura. We think the earth is flat when we look at the house standing here and the yard out there. But that's merely because we're dealing with only a fragment of a circle's or a curve's arc. I'm sure that if you put a number of easy curves in your paths at the camp, you can easily reduce the steepness of the paths to a grade the children can manage readily."

"That's my husband," Mrs. Grace Hansen said proudly. "Glenn, draw her a picture or something. Oh, and am I correct in my assumption we'll not go to San Francisco for dinner? If so, I'll have to plan a celebration dinner and then cook it."

"Mom," Laura asked, "would you mind?"

Her mother wrinkled her nose charmingly.

A few minutes later, in his beautiful oak-paneled study at the rear of the main floor, Dr. Hansen sat down with graphing paper and triangle and pencil and proceeded to show Laura how to plot a path that would carry you up a grade without seeming steep enough to do so. It so happened that Laura was able to draw for him from memory rather close representations of the actual paths at the camp. While she was not able to tell him in terms of percentage how steep the paths were, she was able to give him a fairly good idea by showing him the angle with a ruler and the desk top.

Dr. Hansen's solution of the problem was quite clever. He interconnected the three existing paths with angled lines that carried a person up three or four feet of the grade in about seventy-five feet of travel. A long line slanted upward to the left and then cut back to slant upward to the right and so on. The clever thing was that the three main paths were left intact for use by children and camp workers who were able to ascend the grades without difficulty.

Laura was so thrilled and so pleased she could almost have kissed the squarish-faced, brown-haired, hazel-eyed man who had become her stepfather. End of her major problem! Moreover, he had taught her something she would be able to use all her life. Happily, she took the sheets of graphing paper and folded them carefully and stuck them into the pocket of her cotton shirtwaist dress. "Can do, will do," she said with genuine confidence. "Pop, that's wonderful!"

"Always a pleasure, Laura. May I say something I've been wanting to say ever since you came here? I want to thank you for your consideration for your mother. She was all pins and needles when we flew back from Europe. She felt we should have waited until you had approved our marriage plans. She was afraid—well, that there would be difficulty."

"It's all right."

But those hazel eyes were not eyes readily fooled. "I hope it will be," Dr. Hansen said. "I hope that some day you'll substitute understanding for kindness. But in the meantime, thank you very much for being kind to your mother. I appreciate the fine effort you're making to pretend everything's all right."

Laura, biting her lower lip, wondered how in the world he had discovered she was pretending.

Chapter 12

Laura found it a relief to get back to Camp Mosher. The trouble with a pretense, she discovered, was that you had to be on guard constantly to make certain that you did not betray the pretense to the person to whom you were pretending. She therefore found it very good indeed to be back in her cabin in the Lady Fern Unit where she could be herself. But at the same time she was glad that she had gone home with her mother and spent so much time with Dr. Hansen. She had liked him! It had been easy to talk to him, far easier than she had imagined it would be. In the past she had always been a bit afraid of him because he had been, after all, her mother's employer. But all during yesterday and most of last evening he had been relaxed and friendly and not at all the cold sort of person she had thought him to be.

In fact, Laura thought, changing into camp duds, Dr. Hansen had proven himself to be a very warm if perceptive person.

A hail interrupted Laura's thoughts.

It was Keith Moller.

Stuffing the tails of her blouse down into her shorts, Laura turned her mind to more immediate concerns. She took her time about going outdoors in response to Keith's hail. Also, although this required considerable effort, she managed to greet him very, very casually. Her exact words were, "Oh, it's you, Keith. Hi. How go things in the Deer Fern Unit?"

"Quite well, I'd guess." Quite as if unaware of her casualness, Keith said, "Come see what I've been doing with Mr. Scofield and some of the fellows."

"I'd better check in at the office first. I'm surprised you're here at this hour of the day. Doesn't Beverly Anglin know how to use her assistants?"

Keith just strolled along with Laura. They took the main path that wound around the various clumps of redwoods in an easterly direction through the different divisions. When they neared the administration area, Laura noticed mounds of earth here and there, and then she noticed that all three paths which led up to the recreation hall and mess hall and swimming-pool area had been interconnected by other paths, just as Dr. Hansen had plotted out on graphing paper.

"Works pretty well," Keith said. "I have the testimony of six wheel chair cases to prove that. All girls. Not the strongest girls in the camp, either."

"Keith, how grand!"

"It's an old mountain-climbing trick, you know. Did I ever tell you I like to climb hills and mountains? That sort of thing is called traversing. You zigzag right and left up a steep slope to avoid a practically straight-up climb."

"What a dangerous sport!"

"Anything you do is dangerous, it seems to me. Right now, for instance, we're walking under redwoods. A branch could snap off and hit you on the head. But you don't worry about that happening, do you?"

Laura just had to try the new path arrangement. She went back to Division I and got Miss Canby's permission to borrow a wheel chair not being used. She rolled along the main path to the foot of the grade and then set off along the new path Keith and company had scraped away and dug into the embankment. She found that the ascent by means of this new path was easy, that the only problem was the softness of the earth.

"Natch, we'll blacktop the paths if and when you approve the layout," Keith announced. "Miss Aronstam said this is your project and needs your okay."

"Do it by tomorrow, please?"

"Talk about a whip cracker!"

Laura said evenly, "The best time to do anything is right away. I certainly found that out when my Mom popped in to surprise me. I went straight home with her before I could think up a lot of reasons for a delay. And it all worked out very nicely. Keith, I saw a different Dr. Hansen from anything I've ever seen before."

"You were just afraid of him before, if you ask me. Why not? A mother's boss is a mother's boss."

"It's odd, Keith, but I had the feeling all yesterday that he understands me. Now how can that be? I mean, he hasn't had children; he hasn't been a family man."

"Well, teachers get to know kids pretty well, don't you guess? He's seen a lot of kids come and go, I imagine."

"Keith, you should see my new room! Why, it's a suite, really. First, there's the dreamiest private living room with three gabled windows. Then you go along a little hall that has three huge closets, and you come to a bedroom with an honest-to-goodness fireplace that works. And the bathroom! It has a huge tub and also a shower stall. Keith, when Dr. Hansen said I could have the whole suite, I almost flipped."

"Maybe I should become dean of a junior college instead of a medical doctor."

It seemed to Laura that for just a moment she saw a glitter of jealousy in Keith's blue eyes.

She stopped rolling her chair along the paths.

"I'f I'm not to be afraid of anything any more," she told him, "you're not to be jealous or resentful any more. And it isn't as if I'd done anything special to earn that suite, you know. It's just something given to me. It doesn't make me a more able person than you, does it?"

"Sorry."

Laura saw suddenly that she was not being nearly as casual with Keith as she had planned to be. She was annoyed with herself, but not for long. The truth was, she decided, that she could never be entirely casual with Keith for the simple reason that Keith had gone to a lot of trouble at a critical time in her life to give her a friendly helping hand. So for all the years of their lives, naturally, they would be friends. And how could you be casual in friendship?

"We have a lot to teach one another, I guess," Laura said. "Now isn't that interesting?"

Then onward she rolled and at last came with

a minimum of effort to the broad sweep of ground on which the recreation hall, mess hall and swimming pool had been constructed. She jumped out of the chair, nodding with satisfaction. "From now on," she joked, "you're the camp engineer, Keith Moller, but only if you get all the paving done by tomorrow."

He gave a crisp military salute and said mockingly, "Aye, aye, sir!" He was all silly boy when he left. He hopped into the wheel chair and went rolling down one of the old steep paths, yipping like a cowboy all the way.

Actually, it took seven days for the new paths to be paved. It was not that Keith and his helpers loafed, but simply that only a little bit could be done at a time because the area could *not* be closed off while the work was being performed. To Laura, the last of her administrative problems had been solved, and she was now able to concentrate upon the Rose Davis problem. At the suggestion of Dr. Hansen, she got books about blind people and skimmed through them and made notes on information she thought she could use and then discussed the things she had learned with Miss Humbert. From Miss Humbert she learned that a person engaged in any form of social work had to have a plan of attack, too. "What does this Rose Davis do at this camp for thirty days?" Miss Humbert asked one evening. "Certainly she gets up and eats and swims and talks. But what else? If she rises at six and goes to bed at eight and has an hour's nap, she must have activities of one sort or another to occupy her for about thirteen hours a day. Well, what's her schedule to be?"

Once again, Laura went back to work with paper and pencil. But this work, she learned, was more difficult than the other paper work she had done. She found it extremely frustrating, for instance, to know nothing whatsoever about Rose Davis other than that she was blind. Things would be much simpler, she was convinced, if she knew of any special interests the girl had. But when she mentioned this to Miss Aronstam, the gray head shook and Miss Aronstam said crisply, "You're wrong, you know. Consider, for instance, that I know nothing about the children who are scheduled to come here all summer long. I really don't know anything about them as individuals. As you know, this camp is supported by the Friends of the Crippled Children League, and they scoop up children from all areas of California and ship them to us. I receive names and ages, and that's all. Yet our camp program seems to delight the youngsters. Now why is that?"

"I suppose you mean, ma'am, that all children have basic needs, and you build the program around those needs."

"Right. All children need exercise. All children need amusements. All children need food and shelter and so on. Now you know and I know that not all boys like to play baseball. So, sensibly, we provide the opportunity for the boys to play various games. You see? We figure out a number of things the children can do, and then we allow each child to make his own selection within certain limitations."

Laura gave much thought to that. Then that evening, while she was waiting for Randy to come for his meat scraps, she came to the conclusion that she had really been tackling the problem the wrong way all along. Her mistake, she decided, was in forgetting that, blind or not, Rose Davis was still a girl. Girl things would therefore be of interest to Rose. For instance, Rose would probably just love to dance if a thoughtful partner could be found for her. And who was the dreamiest dancer in the camp?

Paging Clay Chatham!

Randy came, and then Nikki came, too. Nikki looked a mess in mud-spattered jeans and blouse, and she sat down on the porch as if utterly bushed.

"Did you know," Nikki asked dolefully, "that a boy in a wheel chair can run away?"

"Happens every year, Nikki. I think that what motivates them is a longing for high adventure."

"This boy went as far as he could along the Popham Creek trail, and then he just got out of that wheel chair and crawled across the little footbridge and went on. Technically, he wasn't my responsibility, but I was helping Clay out, and Clay wasn't around to go hunting for him."

Nikki sighed.

Laura had an inspiration. "How would you like to come work here, Nikki? I know there are other girls filled with eagerness to become moppet wranglers. I'll need someone to help with Rose Davis. After all, I won't be around twenty-four hours a day seven days a week."

"Nope."

Surprised and just a little bit hurt, Laura asked, "Why not?"

"Every time Clay sees you, he goes swoon-moon-June. May I ask a personal question, as friend to friend?"

"Yes."

"What do you do to Clay?"

Laura had to laugh. "That's the strange thing, Nikki. I don't consciously do anything. I guess it's that old business of gravitation again. People just naturally gravitate toward certain people."

"Seriously," Nikki asked, "would you take me? I wouldn't tell anyone else this, but I'm not too sold on Beverly Anglin. There's a gal who can be mean."

"Mean?"

"Sometimes, Laura, she pinches or slaps the children."

Laura's feet came slamming down from the rail on which she had been resting them. "Nikki," she said scandalized, "that's a terrible accusation to make!"

"I've seen her, Laura."

"But that's hard to believe! I mean, Beverly has been a moppet wrangler for three years, too."

"It's her nerves, I guess. Did you ever wonder why Beverly became rough and tough with you the moment she became unit leader? She's sweet on Keith, and she saw that Keith is sweet on you. So right away Beverly went to work to get you out of the unit. Only that didn't work, did it?"

Laura said, exasperated, "I don't understand people any more. All of a sudden there's so much of this boy and girl stuff. That's ridiculous! We have to get through high school and college and job training and all that. Anyway, there's certainly no place for that nonsense here. It so happens that we have serious responsibilities to these crippled children, and we should think about those first."

"That's easy for you to say, Laura, because you have two swoony admirers. Anyway, if you want me, I'll come running."

Laura said that was fine. Then she gave thought to having a candid talk with Beverly Anglin.

Chapter 13

Rose Davis came early on the morning of August first. She came in an elegant black limousine driven by a uniformed chauffeur, and she was accompanied by a Mrs. Gransbury. Laura first met Rose in Miss Aronstam's office after Mrs. Gransbury had driven away almost the moment she could get away. Laura was puzzled by Mrs. Gransbury's quick departure, but not for long. Right after Miss Aronstam had introduced her to Rose, Rose Davis snapped, "I hate your voice. I hate all soupy sweet voices."

"You'll grow accustomed to it." Laura laughed. "It may even grow on you."

Miss Rose Davis, if you please, spat at Laura's

face.

Peppery Miss Aronstam never said a word in rebuke. After Laura had disgustedly wiped her face with her handkerchief, Miss Aronstam suggested, "Why don't you walk Rose to her cabin, Laura? Oh, and I've approved your request for Nikki's services. I think I'll assign Keith to the Lady Fern Unit, as well. That's a lot of staff for just one person, but this is a basic research project, actually, and there will be more work than two can handle."

Laura reached out and took Rose's arm. Rose snapped at her, "Don't touch me! I can't bear to be touched! Just walk and I'll follow you."

Laura personally doubted that Rose could follow her for long, but her experience at Camp Mosher had long ago taught her to keep all doubts to herself. Very often the children surprised her by doing things she did not believe they could do. She said amiably, "As you wish, Rose. Let's go." She set off slowly, making plenty of noise with her feet so that Rose could locate her by the sounds. She called, "Doorway," as she opened the door, but she let Rose find her own way through the doorway, and she let Rose close the door, too.

Once outdoors, Rose stopped short. She made a queer sound that attracted Laura's attention. Laura turned to see the girl sniffing at the air much as Randy sniffed at the air. Rose moved her head slowly this way and that. Presently she asked, "What's that musky scent?"

"The ferns. They always give off that scent after they've been watered and sprayed. These happen to be giant woodwardia ferns, or western chain ferns. They're clumped up in big circular plantings on each side of this path. Some of the fronds are eight feet tall."

"What's between me and the ferns?"

"Just ground. Not absolutely smooth ground. In the woods, we never rake things perfectly clean and smooth. The trees and the ferns need humus and litter, you see. Just lift your feet a few inches from the ground as you walk, though, and you'll be all right."

Rose surprised Laura by following the suggestion exactly. She also surprised Laura by stopping when she had come within touching distance of the ferns. Only then did Rose raise her hands and reach out to touch one of the fronds.

Interested, Laura asked, "How did you know when to stop, Rose?"

"I just knew."

"There has to be more of an explanation than that."

"Shut up."

And now, with both hands, Rose examined the fern frond. It was fascinating to Laura to watch the girl's fingers. Lightly, delicately, moving in different directions as if each were some kind of antenna, the fingers traced the outlines of the leaves and the frond segments and felt the texture of the leaves on both sides and measured the thickness of the stem. "What color?" Rose asked.

"Medium green but with the green shading just a bit toward yellow. It's always interesting to watch a frond come up. It pokes up from the ground very tightly coiled, and then it uncoils a bit each day, with tiny green leaves on delicate stems. But growth comes very quickly."

"Shut up."

Rose got down on her knees and with her hands rummaged around down at the crown of the root system. Suddenly she laughed. "Is this a frond coming up?" she asked.

Laura looked. "Sure enough. They do that, you know. They seem always to be renewing themselves."

Rose stood up and came back to the path. Smudges of wet earth clung to her skirt, and Laura said, "Here, let me brush you off."

"Don't dare touch me! I won't be touched!"

Patiently, Laura moved on again. They got to the main path with no difficulty, but it took a long, long time. Always, always, always, Rose sniffed the air. Always, always, always, different fragrances or stenches had to be identified. What especially interested Laura was the fact that Rose seemed quite disinterested in sounds. A stellar jay squawked overhead, but Rose asked no question about it. Off in the distance Mr. Scofield began to split a log with a splitting maul, but the rhythmic chunks of the maul into the redwood aroused no curiousity, either. It almost appeared that the girl's most useful apparatus was her nose. And this was sharply at variance with many of the things Laura had read about blind people.

Miss Humbert came to meet them when they reached Division III. Laura made the introductions, but Rose paid no attention. Looking amused rather than annoyed, Miss Humbert gave Laura the V for victory sign, and Laura went on to the Lady Fern Unit with Rose.

"You'll like Miss Humbert," she told Rose. "I think one of the reasons you're here is that Miss Humbert is especially interested in people with your problem."

"Shut up."

Laura, her lips pursed, gave thought to the girl's rudeness. She was quite willing to make allowances for nervousness and even fear. But it seemed to her that Rose was less afraid than she was ill-tempered. Just testing, Laura said quietly, "Don't ever tell me that again, Rose. Don't ever spit at me again, either."

Rose swung around much like a nervous and combative Randy. She actually raised her hands and crooked her fingers like claws.

"You see," Laura told her, "I want you to have a good time here, and there's never much fun when a person spoils things with rudeness."

"Did I ask to come?"

"What's that musky scent, Rose?"

"Woodwardia."

"All right. The only clump of woodwardia in this unit is planted just to the left of our cabin's steps. There are four short but wide steps, then eight feet of porch, then the door. I think you'll like our cabin. We have a wood stove for the cool nights, and we have a raccoon."

Rose sat down with a show of fatigue as soon as she had located a chair on the little porch. "I never mean to be rude," she said. "It's simply that people overdo, and after a while it's irritating."

"In what way do they overdo?"

"Well, they sometimes make a person feel utterly useless. They grab your arm to guide you, as if God didn't give you a sharp nose and sharp ears and a sort of sensitivity to nearby objects."

"If we overdo, it isn't deliberate. A person wants to help. And if we're not blind, how do we know what's necessary and what isn't?"

"I don't like your voice."

"I don't like your manners."

"All right. Send me home. Do you think I care? This is a horrible place! It has bad smells and wild sounds, and I don't like it."

"Doll baby," Laura said, "nothing you can ever do will make me send you home."

About to elaborate, Laura saw Beverly Anglin coming along, big and red-faced and her black eyes flashing. Laura jumped up and went to meet Beverly more than halfway, and Beverly, her hands on her hips, stopped short and waited.

"What's all this about raiding my staff?" Beverly asked. "I think that's a dirty trick."

"I don't see why, Bev. I did train Keith and Nikki, in a way."

"You need three wranglers for one kid? I plan to protest."

"Fine."

"And another thing! Please tell Nikki to watch her tongue if she knows what's good for her."

"Oh?"

"If she wants to leave my unit, that's one thing. But she doesn't have to tell fibs about me."

Just then Keith Moller came along. Beverly hotly ordered Keith to return to the Deer Fern Unit, but Keith waved a slip of paper and said he was a Lady Fern bohunk now. Exasperated, Beverly whirled on her heel and ran off, presumably to protest forthwith.

Grinning, Laura took the transfer slip from Keith. "We have a wilder version of Randy," she warned him, gesturing toward Rose. "I counsel a very careful approach."

The good humor of her lovely face brought a grin to his own. "Can do, will do," he teased. "And may I say, glorious leader, how glad I am to be under your supervision again? I think we should celebrate with a dinner at Scopazzi's."

"Easy come, easy go, as I've said before! I have a better idea. I've been telling the folks about you, and they think a dinner at our place would be nice. Is it all right for a girl to show a boy her personal suite? Honest, you just have to see it, Keith, to believe it."

Rose called, "Where's somebody? I'm bored!"

Keith stepped quickly and confidently to the cabin. "Hi, redhead," he said easily. "What good luck brought you to the Lady Fern Unit?"

"Who are you?"

"Keith Moller. I'm elected to develop hiking trails and such for you. Do you like to hike?"

"You have a nice voice."

"Thanks."

"I hate bossy voices."

Laura, her cheeks tingling, decided she would have to watch her vocal tones in the future. It was very possible, she had to concede, that in her eagerness to get thing done she was sometimes too bossy. Even Keith had once accused her of being a whip cracker!

Rose asked, "What about a hike now? I like to find out everything I can about a place I'm in."

Keith looked at Laura. Laura nodded. A minute later, with Rose holding lightly to Keith's left arm, the two went off along a trail that would eventually take them to Popham Creek. Laura naturally trotted back to the administration area to see to Rose Davis' luggage.

She interrupted a donnybrook!

Nikki McCloud and Beverly Anglin were standing in Miss Aronstam's office, hurling insults at one another. Beverly was calling Nikki a liar, and Nikki was calling Beverly a bully, and there, watching and listening, were Miss Humbert and Miss Aronstam.

Laura's arrival brought quiet for only ten or fifteen seconds, though.

Beverly, as white as a sheet, pointed a trembling finger at Laura and said, "There's the *real* fly in the potato soup. Right from the start she resented being replaced by me, and she's turned Nikki and Keith against me!"

Laura shrank back almost instinctively, taken by surprise.

And Beverly Anglin raged on: "All she can think about is boys and getting what she wants. If you ask me, she's the real disgrace of Camp

Mosher. She left in a huff. And night after night after night she entertains Keith all alone at her cabin."

A queer sensation of sickness came into the pit of Laura's stomach. She said huskily, "That's going to far, Beverly Anglin. First of all, I never entertain Keith in the cabin. We sit outside and watch Randy, and you know it, because you've come spying more than once."

Miss Humbert said firmly to Miss Aronstam, "I personally vouch for the good character of Laura and Keith. I've often gone there to see Randy myself. Anyway, this is really beside the point, if I may say so. I've interviewed some of the children indirectly, and Beverly has slapped several and pinched several."

"The little mutts have to be taught to behave!"

That was Beverly Anglin's big mistake. To Miss Aronstam, children were not mutts to be bullied or mistreated and never would be. "Everyone out except Beverly, please," she requested.

Her tone became harsh.

"You'll run both units," she informed Laura.

'But I think we'll transfer Keith."

About to argue that, Laura changed her mind. This was not the time, she saw, to argue anything with Miss Aronstam.

Chapter 14

Then on Sunday, in her elegant personal suite in the Dean's Residence of Kenyon Junior College, things became even more difficult for Laura. She woke up feeling gloriously refreshed by the night's sleep. In robe and nightgown, she headed for the kitchen to bum an early breakfast from Mrs. Gammage. But her mother was there in the private living room, and there was an odd, pinched expression on her mother's face. Startled, Laura took one of the armchairs. "What's the matter, mother hen?" she asked. "Are you starving, too?"

"I simply thought I'd love to see what you look like."

"Of all the silly things to say!"

"Not really, dear. Mothers do have an interest in their children, and they do like to see their children from time to time."

"I come every weekend, don't I?"

"And avoid me whenever possible. You must never underestimate my powers of observation, dear, or my discernment, for that matter."

Laura tried to keep on meeting her mother's eyes, but failed.

"I have the oddest feeling," Mrs. Hansen said, "that in effect we've signed an armistice. We're not at war, but we're not really at peace, either."

"Mom, *please*. I'm having it rugged at Camp Mosher."

"I'm having it rugged in my own home. You always have time for Glenn, but not for me. We haven't had a decent talk. Your lips say one thing, but your eyes say something else. What am I to do, dear?"

"Mom, it's all right. It's just that it all takes getting used to."

"Then perhaps the process ought to be hurried. We won't have too much time together once the autumn semester begins. What about coming home now so that we may spend some time becoming reacquainted?"

"But I have my obligations!"

"Or are you using your obligations as a type of hiding place?"

"Mom!"

"Laura, we must have this thing out. It exists. We can't pretend otherwise. As intelligent human beings, we—"

"Mom, *you* married the man; I didn't! I was perfectly content with things as they were. But you wanted something else, and you have it. Well, you can't blame me if things have changed. Now can you?"

"Yet you like Glenn. That's rather obvious."

"You bet I do, Mom. But that's just a matter of luck. You could have married someone I might have hated."

"And so we get back to your opinion that I had no right to marry Dr. Hansen unless and until you approved."

Laura wanted to burst from the room and get away, far, far away from any and all problems. All of a sudden she was sick and tired of having problems. Maybe problems helped you to grow up, but right now she was far from sure she wanted to grow up.

"If you wish," Mrs. Hansen said, "you may bring the blind girl here."

"No, ma'am."

"Why not?"

"Mom, regardless of my personal problems, I have to do my duty. We're conducting a very important research project at the camp. A lot depends upon the outcome of that research, and I'm a key figure in the project."

"Very well. But you're quite certain that's how you want it, Laura?"

Something about her mother's manner warned Laura they had come to an important crossroads in their personal relationship. Sensing that words had to be used very carefully now, Laura said, "It isn't a question any more, Mom, of how I want things. Here we are. I didn't make the situation; it was thrust upon me. I'm trying my level best to adjust to it, but it takes time."

"All right. I think I'll go east for a while. There's an important seminar I ought to attend, and Glenn is perfectly willing to let me go alone."

Laura swallowed.

"It's interesting," Mrs. Hansen said. "You've been complaining about Rose Davis' rude refusal to try to learn to adjust. Yet you're quite unable to perceive that in your way you're a Rose Davis, too. I'm afraid, button nose, that I'm not happy about you right now."

And that having been said, Laura's mother left quickly, closing the door firmly behind her.

Laura waited for a while and then went downstairs to the kitchen. She found Dr. Hansen already at the stove, checking on the progress of the ham and eggs Mrs. Gammage was scrambling together. He smiled and winked at Laura. "A slow cook's an abomination," he said, "have you ever noticed?"

"Hi, Pop."

"Hi, Laura."

Laura caught Mrs. Gammage studying her out of the corners of her eyes. Puzzled, Laura went back to the dining room and took her usual chair at the side of the table. Dr. Hansen went upstairs to tell her mother that breakfast was just about ready. When he returned to take his place at the table, his smile was gone.

Feeling guilty, Laura asked, "Pop, what can I do? I haven't made any scenes or anything."

"It's quite all right, Laura."

His voice, of course, informed her that it was far from all right.

So, feeling nervous about it but whispering, "Can do, will do," Laura went upstairs and knocked on the door of the master bedroom. She found her mother just pulling on a lacy slip. Her mother, she thought, had a devastating figure for a woman her age. When her mother's face came poking up out of the slip, Laura suddenly marveled that it had taken her mother all those years to find a second husband. Any objective person on earth, she thought, would say that even now her mother was a beautiful woman. That combination of honey-brown hair and blue-gray eyes and pixie-like smile was alluring, to say the least.

"Breakfast's served," she told her mother. "I guess you could call it a pretty elegant breakfast. Mrs. Gammage made popovers."

"I'm not hungry, thanks."

Her mother went to the wardrobe closet and stood looking at her dresses and suits. She finally took out a light tan linen dress with cap sleeves. She checked the dress in her customary business-like fashion before she put it on.

"Wherever you're going," Laura said, "you should eat something, Mom. If it pains you to eat with me, I'll eat with Mrs. Gammage in the kitchen."

"Oh, pish and tush, dear. I think you misunderstand me. I'm simply not hungry. As for the rest —well, you're quite right, of course. What I did in England was a most foolish thing. I know better than to be impulsive, and I ought to have discussed everything with you before I allowed Glenn to talk me into marriage. Well, the whole thing can be corrected. By this time next week, I'll be moved back into our old residence and all will be as it was before."

"*What?*"

"I suppose I was disturbed and angry earlier this morning because I suspected I would have to decide to divorce Glenn. I wasn't brought up to think of marriage as anything but a forever arrangement. It's often disturbing, as you'll some day find, to be constrained to take action not in conformance with the dictates of your earlier training. But—"

"Is that why Pop's looking practically sick at the table? Did you tell him your plans?"

"Had to. You see, Laura, you've been quite wrong in one highly important respect. Ever since you came along, you've been uppermost in my thoughts and emotions, I assure you. That's how things are. To me, you come first. So if I must choose between hurting you and hurting Glenn, naturally I'll hurt Glenn. I won't like doing it, because I don't think people should hurt others. But if I have no other option, I'll do it."

Laura had to sit down. She took the small chair near the windows and looked longingly out at the day. She wished achingly that she could be out there in the lovely sunshine with nothing more major on her mind than whether to go swimming or do some gardening. And the odd thing was that the knowledge that her mother put her first was no help at all. All she could really think about was the sick expression on the face of the man she had left at the breakfast table. He had been so happy when she had come home yesterday and had kissed him in greeting and had dragged him off to his study to brief about about the big events of the week at Camp Mosher. And now?

"Wool gathering or daydreaming never helps," Mrs. Hansen said gently. "All this will be difficult and painful for a few weeks, but facing up to facts and doing one's best to live with facts is really best in the end. I just want to say one thing about Glenn to you, Laura, and then we'll drop the subject permanently. Glenn is a splendid man. After your father died, money was a major problem. At that time, Glenn was superintendent of the Kenyon school system. When he heard of your father's death, he got in touch with me and said there was always a position waiting for me if I needed one. So I returned to teaching. And Glenn made it possible for me to do graduate work and take my master's. When the post developed here, Glenn arranged an interview with old Dean Mikel, and I was invited to join the faculty. So, you see, even though I may have been somewhat impulsive in England, I had known Glenn a long, long time, and I knew him to be a very kind, thoughtful, generous man the two of us could depend upon in any emergency. All right. Any questions before we drop the matter?"

Laura's biggest need just then was a chance to think not a chance to ask questions. She simply shook her head and turned her gaze back to the windows.

"Very well," her mother said gravely. "Now as to the future: if you will get your personal things together, I'll arrange for them to be taken back to our old residence. It might be well for you to take extra clothes to the camp this week. I won't have time to see to them the next two weeks. There, how do I look?"

And she turned slowly for Laura's inspection, quite as if she had not just decided to do so ghastly a thing as to blight a fine man's life forever.

Laura was shocked and angry and hurt for Dr. Hansen and hurt for herself. "You look very beautiful," she said.

"Fine. Always look beautiful, dear. It does so much for your morale."

Grace Hansen blew her a kiss, picked up her handbag and started vivaciously toward the door.

Laura called out, knowing she had to: "Wait, Mom. Mom, please wait."

Her mother stopped with her hand on the doorknob.

"You're doing all this just for me, Mom?"

"Well, you're my only child, after all. I certainly want you to be happy. I certainly don't want a permanent wall between us. Well, let's say that I've goofed, to use your term. Now I'm correcting the goof. And if I've been able to forgive your goofs in the past, then you ought to be able to forgive this goof now."

"It isn't a question of forgiveness, Mom. I guess I just never paid much attention to things like money and your job and how lonely you must have been and all."

"Your father and I had a beautiful life together, Laura. You know that, I'm sure. After he left us, things would have seemed pointless to me, except for you. I never expected to remarry. There we were, and we seemed to be doing all right. But it would appear that I had a need for Glenn and he for me. And in all frankness, I think you missed a great deal, growing up without a lord and master in the house. I felt well, no matter what I felt, eh?"

Laura made a decision. She stood up and said as firmly as she could, "I can't let you do this to Pop, Mom. He's too nice."

Her mother sat down on the bed.

Laura went to her and threw her arms around her fiercely. And there was much more than just kindness in the hug. Back in a great glorious flood came all the pride and love she had ever had for her mother.

"Darn it," Laura scolded, "why didn't you tell me about all those problems long ago? Why didn't you tell me what a wonderful, helpful friend Dr. Hansen was?"

"Time enough for girls to have problems when they're grown, dear. I've never had much respect for people who wail about their problems."

"All right! Now no more gloom and fears and tears. We're alive! What do we have to fear?"

"Then you want to try again," with no walls between us; with none of that obvious kindness to a poor old lady?"

"Mom, I wasn't that obvious, was I?"

"Well . . . sometimes. Of course, I do give you an A for having tried to be kind."

"You have to be kind. Take Rose Davis at the camp. When she spat on my face, it was all I could do not to slap her. But it was so obvious that she was nervous and scared silly and unhappy and—hey, I'm *starving.*"

They hustled downstairs.

Dr. Hansen had left the table and gone into his study. He looked puzzled and distraught when they popped in on him, but laughing kisses delivered by his female kith and kin changed his expression in a hurry.

"I'll never understand women," he said. "Never!"

Chapter 15

Laura returned to camp the following morning in a joyous frame of mind. She kissed Nikki and Rose hello and would probably have kissed Clay Chatham, too, had she not feared there would be a great scandal. As it was, she pumped Clay's hand up and down and said, "Welcome to the unit, old son, and if you hop or pop to me just once, I'll sick Randy onto you."

"What's cranked you up?" Clay asked. "Not that a fellow minds. Why should he mind? It wouldn't be logical. All girls should be pretty, right? Being cranked up has made you pretty, right? So I cheer whatever it was that cranked you up. Like I said: logical!"

Laura turned from him, laughing, and went over to the Dear Fern Unit to take over its control once more. She would have a total staff of four now, she soon discovered. Two moppet wranglers she did not recognize were already at work getting the children assembled at the work benches in the big redwood grove. Laura just stood by casually and watched proceedings. Division III would certainly be a catch-all division for problem cases, she saw. One of the children was practically a lie-down case, her little body encased from chest to toes in a thick plaster cast. Puzzled, Laura looked at Clay. "How did the wrangler get that youngster into that wheel chair? I didn't think she was strong enough to handle such loads."

"I lifted and she directed. It'll be a good system, boss lady. Now that we have boys and girls in the same unit, there'll always be a fellow around to help with the heavy work."

"I think I ought to have another boy here, Clay. There are seven cabins in this unit. We could have a maximum of forty-two campers in this unit alone. Two girls to handle the girls, two boys to handle the boys. I'll speak to Miss Humbert about that."

His gray eyes narrowed. "Don't tell me you miss Keith already."

Laura just reached out and patted his face soothingly. "I live only for Clay Chatham," she teased, "how's that?"

Made sheepish by the tomfoolery, Clay went into the grove to help the wranglers get the children started on their arts and crafts projects.

It seemed to Laura that now was as good a time as any to launch Rose Davis' camping experience. She sent Nikki off to fetch the girl, and she made a place for Rose at the head of a table at which older children happened to be sitting. She introduced herself to the wranglers and she then outlined her general thinking on the subject of how Rose ought to be handled. Marjorie Mendenhall, a plump, tomboyish girl dressed in denim pedal-pushers and a pullover green terry-cloth blouse, reported that arts and crafts were her special love and that she hoped to be an arts and crafts teacher. On a hunch, Laura requested her to dream up a simple project for Rose, and then Laura went off to sit on a log to await developments.

Rose came along with Nikki, protesting almost every foot of the way. "I hate projects," Rose said over and over again. "Why won't people just leave me alone?"

Marjorie stepped over to Rose and made the error of taking Rose by the hand. Rose snatched her hand away and screeched that she hated to be touched. Marjorie laughed heartily and announced, "Do tell! Now you listen to me, Red. You could break your neck trying to get through this tangle of wheel chairs and benches and crutches unaided. So when you're in my group, you let me make these big decisions, okay?"

"I hate you!"

"Baloney!" Marjorie retorted. "You just hate yourself, that's all. And I wonder why. If I had your snappy figure and that glorious red hair, I know I'd love myself."

And Marjorie took her hand again and very

briskly led Rose to her seat at the head of the table.

Inevitably, all action and all conversation was stopped by the other children. Inevitably, all eyes were aimed at the head of the table. People were always interested in the novel, of course, and the crippled children of the Deer Fern Unit were no exception. Laura was interested to observe that, because she knew that practically all crippled children resented it when they were stared at by well people who thought crippled people were unusual. It all depended, Laura reasoned, upon the point of view!

"We'll make a pottery dish," Marjorie told Rose in a voice of great authority. "I notice you have long, slender, very sensitive fingers. That's fine, because if you have sensitive fingers, you can't commit the goof of making your finish too lumpy or the edges of your dish too thick or too thin. Have you ever made a pottery dish?"

Rose put her hands on her lap. "'You can't make me slave," she said. "I dare you!'"

"Well, there's a lovely ball of green clay in

front of you," Marjorie said. "Also, there are tools for inscribing a design on the dish after the dish has been formed. If you want to work, go ahead. If not, just enjoy the sounds of all these other monsters huffing and puffing away like eager beavers without teeth."

All the other children in the grove chuckled or laughed, and then one boy said very loudly that he did so have teeth, even if he probably would not keep them for long. Marjorie demanded a look at his teeth, and sure enough, she found an upper front tooth that was somewhat wobbly. "Well, that's how it is with your first teeth," Marjorie said. "In they come; out they go."

A girl asked why that was.

Marjorie confessed that she did not know.

Amazingly, Rose said at the head of the table, "Your first teeth are called deciduous teeth because you shed them as you get older, just like deciduous trees shed their leaves every year. Your first teeth are very important because they help to shape your mouth. If your mouth isn't properly shaped by the time your permanent teeth come out to replace your deciduous teeth, you have trouble."

A girl sitting beside Rose asked worriedly if her mouth were shaping up properly. Rose reached out, and her delicate fingers moved about the girl's mouth. No one made a sound. Even Laura moved closer to the table, the better to watch. Next, Rose moved her fingers to follow the curves of the girl's cheeks to her cheekbones. What she was doing, apparently, was using her fingers to get some idea of the shape of the girl's face. The fingers went lightly all over the girl's face, and the girl, watching with wide gray eyes, never moved a muscle until Rose had quite finished.

"You're very pretty," Rose said to the girl, "aren't you?"

The girl was fascinated. "I am?"

"I predict that when you grow up, all the boys will follow you wherever you walk. I predict that when you grow up you'll have to dance so many dances at a party that—"

"I've got no legs," the girl interrupted. "Mommie said never to go on the railroad tracks, but I did, and a train cut my legs off."

"You're teasing me! I hate to be teased! Don't you dare tease me again!"

"Mommie says you should never tease dogs or cats or canaries or ducks or people. You want to feel my leg stumps. But don't tickle so much!"

Rose reached out and down. Laura almost intervened to save everyone embarrassment, but then she recalled having read somewhere that it was good for handicapped people to realize they were not the only people with problems.

Rose snatched her hands away. Her full lips quivered. After a while Rose said, "I don't hate you any more. What's your name?"

"You'll laugh."

"Honest, I won't laugh."

"Everybody says that, but everybody laughs."

"Try me out!"

"You'll laugh."

Interestingly, Rose reached next for the ball of clay on the table. She squeezed here, pressed there, poked around with a fingertip. The ball of clay turned into a miniature clay head! "Guess who?" she asked the girl.

"Hey, you're making *me!* Everybody, she's making *me!*"

"Who are you, I wonder?"

"Cheerfully Rollingstone."

Laura had to give Rose credit. Rose did not laugh. True, when Rose spoke she did so in a very breathy and quivery voice, but Rose definitely did not laugh. "Well, Cheerfully," she said, "let's make a bust of you."

"But I don't *want* to be a bust! Mommie says that stumps or no stumps, I've got to be a success."

"The bust I'm talking about is the model of your head I'll make in this clay."

"You're blind. You can't see nothing. How can you make *me* like that?"

"Fingers see if they're trained to see."

"Huh!"

The delicate fingers of Rose Davis worked on and on and on. No one else was doing any work, but neither Laura nor Marjorie let that bother them. Rose was keeping the children entertained and happy, and the happiness of the children was the main thing. After about a half-hour, Rose reached out and with her fingers examined Cheerfully's face again. "Naturally," she said, "I'd not know what color to make your hair or face or eyes unless you told me. But that doesn't matter when you're making a bust or a statue. All that matters is that I get your features just so."

Rose picked up one of the clay modeling tools. Very, very deftly Rose corrected the little nose she had pinched out with her fingertips. Next, Rose went to work on the mouth.

"Do you know why I'm named Cheerfully Rollingstone?" Cheerfully asked. "I'll tell you because you didn't laugh. Mommie says a rolling stone gathers no moss, and Mommie says it's too bad not to have no moss, but if that's how God wants it, then a rolling stone ought to be cheerful about it. And so I'm Cheerfully Rollingstone."

Rose held the clay head up and asked, "How's this now?"

All the children compared the model head and

face with the head and face of Cheerfully Rollingstone. The likeness was fantastically good, Laura
thought.

Cheerfully said, "I guess it's me, all right.
Can I have me?"

"All right. But it should be dried and lac-
quered. That way, it'll keep a long time."

Marjorie had an inspiration. "Red, she asked,
"I wonder if you'd help me teach some of these
children to work with clay?"

Rose scowled. You could all but hear a loud
and nasty no forming on the tip of her tongue.
But Cheerfully said, "Whee, hurrah for Rose!"
All the children cheered and if Rose ever did say
no, it was unheard. When the cheering had ended,
Rose said in a gentler voice that Laura had ever
heard her use, "I guess if you want me to, all
right. But never scold me! I hate to be scolded!"

Chapter 16

The next afternoon an even more interesting thing happened and revealed to Laura still another facet of Rose Davis' personality and basic character. Like all the patients and teen-agers who camped at Camp Mosher, Laura had lain down at one-fifteen for her customary nap. On this occasion Laura fell into a sound sleep. When the wake-up music blaring through all the public-address loudspeakers had succeeded in wakening her, Laura discovered that Rose Davis was gone. Disturbed, Laura dressed hurriedly and went looking for Rose over in the Deer Fern Unit. Nikki greeted her, chuckling. "If you want to see the sweetest sight, boss lady, hie yourself to Popham Creek."

"Since when have I become known as boss lady?"

"Since you became the boss of two units."

"Well, there's only one patient in the Lady Fern Unit. If I can find her, that is. Have you seen Rose?"

"Rose happens to be the sweet sight you'll see at Popham Creek."

Laura trotted off along the path. She noticed that Clay had strung a guide rope alongside the path for Rose to cling to as she took a hike through the woods. Laura promptly closed her eyes and closed her hand over the guide rope to get some idea of how well Clay had done his work. She discovered two things of interest to her. First, she discovered, you had to be certain to lift your feet as you went along; otherwise you would catch a shoetip in a protruding tree root or a clump of ferns and debris. The second thing she discovered was that the woods seemed quite different when your eyes were closed. She noticed almost at once that there were many, many more sounds in a woods that she had ever realized. There was the sound of the wind strumming through the great redwood trees; and the wind made other sounds, too—the rustling of shrubs leaves, for example, and the knockings of boughs against one another. And there were bird sounds and insect sounds and water sounds!

And *screeching* sounds.

Laura opened her eyes and raced ahead, sure that Rose had fallen into the creek. But when she reached the creek, she found Rose and Cheerfully sitting in just their underwear in the water, having a splash fight. The screechings were pouring from Cheerfully's mouth, because it was an even contest and Cheerfully was having a ball. Laura laughed until tears formed in her eyes and her stomach muscles began to ache. She sat down on a rock and just watched and laughed until both battlers were worn out. When Cheerfully had crawled up to the sunny shore she said purringly, "Here, kitty, kitty, kitty." Rose, not resentful of the teasing or her handicap, at once followed the sound of Cheerfully's voice and threw herself down beside Cheerfully to dry off in the sunshine.

"Of course," Laura said, "you're probably scandalizing everybody in the camp. Bra and panties! What sort of bathing costume is that?"

The two happy kids just giggled and wriggled around like puppies in the warm sunshine.

"We have a deal," Cheerfully told Laura. "Rose carries me on her back, and I steer her. If I pull her left ear, she goes left, and if I pull her right ear, she goes right."

"Isn't she rather heavy for you, Rose?" Laura asked.

"No."

"Chop off your legs and save weight," Cheerfully said. She looked down at her stumps. "I'm gonna have artificial legs pretty soon, though," she bragged. "They're gonna be State of California legs. I guess not everybody can have genuine State of California legs, either."

"I have genuine State of California talking books," Rose told her. "It's interesting. People who write books read them especially for blind people, and then the State of California lends you the records and the phonograph to play them."

"What do you read about?"

"Birds, for instance. There's a set of records that teaches you how to identify birds."

Laura's mind flew back to the day Rose had come and had shown an intense interest in smells but had showed no interest in the squawking of a stellar jay. Laura listened, and when she heard a jay squawk in the distance she asked, "What's that bird?"

Rose asked in turn, "Which one?"

"Which one? I just hear—" And then Laura stopped short, because she heard a piping sound.

"The squawk is a stellar jay," Rose said, "and the other sound is a water ouzel."

Cheerfully bragged, "Rose can hear anything, can't you, Rose?"

Rose smiled faintly. "Well, not everything."

Cheerfully turned excitedly to Laura. "Miss Laura," she asked, "can Rose and me live together?"

"Well, I'll have to think about that, girls.

There isn't room in our cabin for anyone else, and—"

"Miss Laura?"

It was Rose who had interrupted in such a polite tone that Laura found it difficult to believe the same Rose had more than once told her to shut up.

"Yes, Rose?"

"Why can't I live in the other unit in the same cabin with Cheerfully? I don't need to be watched or helped all the time."

Laura was touched by the tender way Cheerfully looked at Rose. Glory be, she thought, the moppets had become fast friends!

"Well," she said to them, "suppose we strike a bargain. You guys get into your clothes and behave, and I'll make the transfer this afternoon. Fair enough?"

Cheerfully whooped it up. Rose, on the other hand, began to cry.

Be a unit leader, Laura thought, and meet all kinds and observe all reactions!

She trailed the kids back to the Deer Fern

Unit. They were dripping water and were tired and sunburned, but never once were they cross with one another during the long trip back. Rose stumbled once, and Cheerfully yelled: "Timber!" and both girls put their hands out to break the fall. Then, on the ground, they giggled as if they had had fine sport.

In other words, Laura thought later on while en route to Miss Humbert's cabin, there was really nothing essentially wrong with Rose that being wanted and needed could not correct. If that were true, she thought, the camp ought to put high on its list next year some sort of policy that would guarantee that each blind girl or blind boy would feel wanted and needed. Or could she really make such a recommendation on the basis of her observations of just one blind person?

Her visit caught Miss Humbert having a bath. When Miss Humbert popped out into the living room about five minutes later, she looked damp and steamy and she smelled of soap. Laura liked seeing Miss Humbert with her hair down, so to speak. When Miss Humbert had her hair down, there was little to distinguish her from the moppet wranglers except, maybe, fuller legs and bosoms. Certainly when she had her hair down Miss Humbert was easier to talk to.

"I've put Rose in Cabin No. 5 with Cheerfully Rollingstone," she told Miss Humbert directly. "I caught both of them sitting in their scanties in Popham Creek, and they were having a scrumptious time and asked if they could bunk together."

"I wonder if that would be a good idea, Laura."

"I think so, Miss Humbert. Rose claims that she doesn't need to be watched or helped all the time."

"Oh, I'm not arguing with your basic thesis, dear. I believe, as you seem to believe, that handicapped people can do much for themselves if allowed to. I'm thinking in terms of Rose Davis' temperament. I know the two girls have hit it off well together. But what would happen, I wonder, if for some reason or another Rose became disappointed in Cheerfully? At this stage in her development, Rose is rather scatty. It's purr or scratch, talk gently or spit. I doubt she's ready to participate in the give and take of a unit cabin."

"Well, ma'am, I've made the move. I guess it was an arbitrary thing to do, but they were so eager."

"You're right," Miss Humbert said. "It was arbitrary. Now move Rose back to your cabin, please. I'll not have her spend a night in the other cabin."

Miss Humbert's attitude left Laura with the feeling that she had pulled another one of her goofs. But because Miss Humbert looked at her watch impatiently, Laura did not argue the matter. "Can do, will do," she said amiably.

"Oh, and one thing more, Laura. We can hardly encourage the girls to sit around the creek in their underwear. Punish Rose and Cheerfully by keeping them entirely separated all day tomorrow. Explain to them, please, that rules are rules."

Not too happy about the assignment, Laura nevertheless did as she was told. Much to her surprise, both Rose and Cheerfully took the news well. But their good-humored reactions to the news should have warned Laura to keep a sharp eye on them.

The next morning, Rose was missing from the cabin. Laura zipped over to the Deer Fern Unit, and there, sure enough, were Rose and Cheerfully sound asleep in Cheerfully's bunk.

Twice during the rest of that day, Rose and Cheerfully somehow got together.

And that night, as Laura was locking the door, Rose said sharply, "You can't keep me a prisoner, Miss Laura. You may think so, but you're wasting your time."

"For Pete's sake, will you not make things so difficult for me? I'm doing this for your own good. Perhaps if you accept your punishment like ladies, I can talk Miss Humbert into changing her mind."

"But Cheerfully leaves next Tuesday, Miss Laura. Don't you see?"

Laura did understand. But orders were orders, plague take it.

The next morning both Rose and Cheerfully were missing!

And who found them some three hours later

after the whole camp had been upset?

Keith Moller, of course.

When Keith came back with the girls, Miss Aronstam was on the verge of telephoning the Santa Cruz County sheriff's office. She was saying in typical peppery fashion, "When I see those young ladies, I'll reprimand them most severely."

Naturally, she did nothing of the kind. Instead, she saw to it that the girls were given a special breakfast in the mess hall, and then she summoned Laura and Miss Humbert to her office for a conference.

Miss Aronstam asked just one question. "Why?'

Miss Aronstam asked just one question. "Why?" she asked. "Why?"

Laura allowed Miss Humbert to do all the explaining. Miss Humbert was very fair, telling Miss Aronstam she had made her decision to separate the girls even though Laura had granted them permission to live together. Miss Humbert explained her reason for doing this, and Miss Aronstam nodded as if she agreed.

"And yet," Miss Aronstam then said, "it's always possible to learn from failure as well as from success. For instance, Miss Humbert, suppose Rose does become disappointed in Cheerfully and does turn sour again? We'll have learned something important. For instance, we'll have learned that good friends of today can be bitter enemies tomorrow. But we know that already. For example, we know that Laura here actually turned on her own mother, and—"

"Not really!" Laura protested, shocked.

"In a way so real, young lady, that you came closer than you'll ever know to ruining your mother's happiness. But that's neither here nor there. The point I would make, Miss Humbert, is that we also know that bitter enemies of today can be good friends tomorrow. The fact is, I think it would be interesting to let Rose live with the whole group and exchange in the usual give and take of normal social relationships with her own age group."

"A child must learn discipline somewhere, Miss Aronstam. To be truthful, I hoped that Rose would accept her disappointment patiently and cheerfully. Then I would have returned her to the Deer Fern Unit at once. I just don't want to have her come apart at the seams when Cheerfully leaves next week."

"Well, you're certainly right on that point, Miss Humbert. Discipline is discipline, after all. But would you be willing, do you think, to change your mind about everything if I told you Rose is leaving next week, also?"

"Leaving?" Laura asked.

"Her family is moving east," Miss Aronstam said rather regretfully. "I think it would be nice, all in all, if Rose had the opportunity during these few remaining days to share a cabin with the one friend she appears to have found on earth."

Miss Humbert said quickly. "Of course, Miss Aronstam."

Laura was both flabbergasted and annoyed. "It seems to me," she said, moved by very strong feelings, "that it's downright cruel to take Rose away just when she's beginning to discover she's not the only person in the world with a handicap.

I'd just love to tell her family that. I mean, I really would!"

Miss Aronstam smiled at her just a bit fondly. "You've taken hold of yourself rather well," she complimented her. "I must confess I was a bit worried about you back in early July. Good for you. But as for letting you go to San Francisco to argue with her parents—well, I can scarcely do that without your parents' permission. I do have certain funds available for emergencies, of course. But—"

Laura stopped the director of Camp Mosher right then and there. "Ma'am," she said, standing up grimly, "I'm going to San Francisco if I have to *walk*. If I didn't care about helping people, I wouldn't be here, and I certainly wouldn't let them spit at me without wishing they hadn't!"

And Laura Gray rushed out to look for Keith.

Chapter 17

At ten-fifteen, when Laura got home, she found her mother muttering and sputtering at a sewing machine she had set up in the dining nook in the kitchen. "Button nose," her mother said, "how dare you grow up? When you grow up you make work for a mother hen! Elegant drapes! Elegant bedspread! And do you know what the Mighty Hero is doing? He's going over the family bank account to see if we can't afford to furnish that grown-up suite of yours properly."

"Whee!"

"I'll take a kiss."

Laura gave her one to say hello, another to console the poor decrepit thing, and still another because she was more stirred than she would ever let on.

Then, matter-of-factly, Laura dropped her little bombshell. "Keith and I are driving to San Francisco on a vital matter," she announced. "Could you lend me some money until I get my next pay check?"

"Go ask the Mighty Hero. Mine not to reason why; mine but to stitch or die."

"Do you mean I can go?"

"I mean, go ask the Mighty Hero if you *may* go. Let's watch our language around here. I may be an English teacher no longer, but it's always possible you may want to end up as one."

"Nope. I've definitely decided to get into administration. But how can you give up your work?"

"For two reasons. My husband, your new father, thinks it's time you had a mother around the house on other than a hit-and-miss basis. I agree. Junior year is just ahead! It's a key year in the life of any teen-ager, and especially in the life of a girl. This is the year when sniffy-nosed childhood is cast away forever. A girl begins to discover boys! A girl begins to connive and primp for dances! Also—"

Grace Hansen broke off, because her daughter was giggling and blushing, all excited.

"You'll find the Mighty Hero," Mrs. Hansen said presently, "in his study."

There he sat at the desk, lips pursed, pencil flying over paper. Laura's sudden appearance made him start. His first words went straight to her heart. "Always a pleasure," he said gruffly, a bit embarrassedly. "Is that a car you drove up in?"

"Keith's, Pop. We have a vital errand to do in San Francisco. Just the same, vital or not, I have to have permission to take off."

"Well, your mother—"

"I guess you're the boss around here," Laura said. "I'm to get money and permission from you. I'll pay back the money as soon as I get my pay check."

His brows came together over his nose. He said, "Hm, and then he gave an odd laugh and said, "The things you're not told when a woman agrees to marry you. So I'm the boss, eh? Hm."

Laura sat down and waited as patiently as she could for him to recover from the shock. This man she called Pop, she decided, was really a terribly cute person for a person so old. What with learning to live with a father in the house and learning to connive and primp for all those junior prom dances, this ought to be one of the most interesting school years of her life. But in the meantime—Rose!

"Tell me what it's about, please," Dr. Hansen said. "I'm not terribly anxious, let me tell you, to see you head off to San Francisco with Keith at the wheel of that car."

"He's a good driver, Pop."

"Hm."

"And a girl couldn't possibly be safer than she is under Keith's watchful eye. I may as well tell you here and now, Pop, that I like Keith very much."

"Hm."

Finally Laura got around to telling him what the vital errand was about.

The next thing Laura knew, Dr. Hansen was telling the telephone operator to ring the number of the Carl Davis family in San Francisco. When he got hold of Mrs. Davis, he told Laura to take over, and Laura, keeping her fingers crossed, did.

"Mrs. Davis," she began the conversation, "this is Laura Gray—Laura Gray *Hansen*, that is, the leader of the unit your daughter is staying in at Camp Mosher."

Mrs. Davis said in a gravelly voice, "So?"

"So I must tell you, Mrs. Davis, that I think it would be a perfectly ghastly thing to take Rose out of the camp at this time. She has a friend, a nice girl named Cheerfully Rollingstone who—"

"Nobody can be named that. You think I'm nuts?"

"Well, she's named that, and Rose wants to share the cabin with her, and I want to keep Rose until Labor Day, and I think it's terrible that she has to leave."

"You mean," Mrs. Davis asked, as if she could not believe her ears, "you *want* to keep Rose until Labor Day? Hasn't she spit at your face or scratched at your eyes or kicked your shins?"

"Well, she did spit at me," Laura had to admit, "but that's only because she was afraid and lonely. She doesn't do that any more."

"What are you—a miracle worker?"

"Nope. Just a moppet wrangler, ma'am. I'm simply fascinated by Rose, though, and what I'm trying to do now is study her so that next year the camp can have a real program for blind people. Ma'am, I wish I could talk to you face to face, but I guess my father doesn't want me to drive to San Francisco with Keith because Keith is only sixteen and four months."

"I should say not! Anyhow, there'll be time enough for us to talk later. Look, if you're sure the camp won't care I'd be glad to let you keep Rose until the day after Labor Day. We have to go east on business, and we can't get back until Labor Day. That's why we were taking Rose early. We thought she'd have to leave Camp Mosher the end of August."

"Ma'am, how wonderful! Will you just tele-phone the League lady there in San Francisco?"

Shiny-eyed, Laura returned the telephone handset to the standard. She sat down, wagging her lovely head. "A girl has to do more thinking," she said. "It should have occurred to me to use the telephone."

"Sometimes, when one becomes excited, say, it's rather difficult to think intelligently. It's for that reason, probably, that most people will tell you it's always wise to keep cool."

"I guess I'm like that, Pop. I get steamed up about things."

"It's a matter of developing control. Control comes with practice. But you mustn't fall into the error of thinking it's wrong to believe passionately in some worth-while thing—an ideal of service, let's say. I was proud of you while you were talking to Mrs. Davis. You care passionately about what happens to that blind girl, don't you?"

"Natch."

"Natch?"

"Natch. Do you want to know what I really thought deep, deep down when she spit at me, Pop? I thought angry thoughts, yes. But a part of my mind said there was no difference between her spitting at me and my nasty thoughts aimed at you and Mom. Pop, this may seem crazy to you, but all Rose is, basically, is any girl who's afraid of something or resentful of something. Rose spits. I put a gleam of fear into Mom's eyes. Another girl does something else. See? It's just that different girls have different ways of showing their fears or resentment."

"Well . . ."

"Or a girl," Laura said ashamedly, "makes a man look awfully sick at the breakfast table. Pop, I never apologized for that, did I?"

"No apology necessary. Now let's discuss something quite important. I happen to know that Camp Mosher does close down its season on September first. What do we do about Rose?"

"Some kids stay until Labor Day, Pop, to close the camp for the year. I guess I could stay there with Rose."

"What about bringing Rose to stay with us? I'm interested in her. Also, I think it would be grand if we all had a week or so together before the school year begins."

Laura liked the idea. Still—

"I don't know what Mom would say," she told him dubiously. "I—"

"She would say, I'm sure, that I'm the boss around here."

"Why, she *did* say that, didn't she?"

"Fine. Now go somewhere and let me finish my financial work. It seems that you must have a suite appropriate to your age and position. If we're to have everything in order before the first of the month, we'll have to stop wasting time. I'll want you here Sunday at nine o'clock sharp. We'll drive to some furniture stores I know in the San Jose area and have you pick out what you want. How's that?"

"Whee!"

All battles won, Laura rushed back to Keith in the car. She gave him the news and was thrilled to see a kind of awe come into his eyes. At the same time, though, she found it impossible to accept from Keith, of all people, credit for something she really had not done all alone.

"It isn't Laura Gray Hansen who gets results," she said. "It's the entire Hansen family. Keith, isn't it strange how things sometimes work out? I mean, I was behaving to my folks as Rose behaves to other folks. I guess Rose and I have been afraid of the same thing, afraid of not being wanted. Brother, how wacky can you get? Everyone is wanted by someone when you get right down to it. Brother!"

Keith drove to Kenyon. He parked at the beach, and they got out and went to the water's edge.

"Clay's a nice guy," Keith said. "I like to think I'm nicer, but I guess I'm not. So if you really want him in that unit instead of me, that's all right."

"Sweet of you to tell me," Laura teased. Then something in his eyes told her this was not the time for teasing, so she looked out over the water and said without a tremble in her voice, "I can't think of anyone nicer than you, Keith. Every time I need your help, there you are. It's wonderful to know somebody as generous and loyal as that."

He sat down beside her on the sand.

Laura turned to look at him. She had to. "Keith," she asked, "let's always be friends?"

"Can do, will do."

Laura nodded. Then, there in the warm sunshine, she relaxed for the first time since she had received that letter from her mother in England. It would all be all right now, she thought. Mom and Pop would live happily forever after. Rose Davis would find other friends as good and true as Cheerfully Rollingstone.

And what about Keith Moller and Laura Gray Hansen?

A sparkle came into Laura's eyes, the sparkle of confidence, the sparkle of anticipation. So the junior year was the key year of a teen-ager's life?

Gazing out at the ocean, the eternally sounding ocean, Laura asked, "Aren't we lucky to be alive?"

It seemed to her, though she could not be sure, that the ocean rumbled back: "Yes!"